SHELBY'S S~~A~~

Slick Rock 7

Becca Van

MENAGE EVERLASTING

Siren Publishing, Inc.
www.SirenPublishing.com

A SIREN PUBLISHING BOOK
IMPRINT: Ménage Everlasting

SHELBY'S SAVIORS
Copyright © 2012 by Becca Van

ISBN: 978-1-62241-953-1

First Printing: November 2012

Cover design by Les Byerley
All art and logo copyright © 2012 by Siren Publishing, Inc.

Printed in the U.S.A.

PUBLISHER
Siren Publishing, Inc.
www.SirenPublishing.com

DEDICATION

I would like to dedicate this book to my very own hero.

Honey, you have been at my side through all the ups and downs and have been my pillar of strength. You continue to bolster me through my illness, and for that I will be forever grateful. You are my sanity as well as my breath.

I love you so much. xxoo

SHELBY'S SAVIORS

Slick Rock 7

BECCA VAN
Copyright © 2012

Chapter One

"Fuck me, would you look at that," Cord rasped. He'd never seen the woman walking down Slick Rock's main street before, but she was captivating. Her hair was a combination of many colors, and all of them were totally natural from what he could tell. There were rich browns, lighter ones as well, and tints of red, gold, and blonde, which seemed to capture light within the strands.

Beside him, his brother Brandt said, "Whoa." Both men stopped in their tracks and watched the woman heading into the diner across the street from the building that housed their cousins' security company.

Cord exchanged a look with Brandt. They'd intended to head over to the Slick Rock Hotel after a long day of work, but sitting around in the lobby didn't seem half as interesting as it had a moment ago.

Without a word, they changed direction and followed the woman to the diner.

Cord took the booth opposite the young woman and watched her from the corner of his eye. She was such a sexy little thing, no more than five foot one but voluptuous enough to suit his and his brother's tastes. He wanted to know the color of her eyes and what her name was, but he didn't want to be too forward and put her on alert.

The waitress came and took her order, and the sound of the woman's light, feminine voice sent shivers racing up and down his spine, causing goose bumps to erupt all over his skin. Physically restraining himself from going over there and asking her name was one of the hardest things he'd ever had to do. Cord had never felt so drawn to a woman before, and from the looks his brother was giving her, he felt the same way.

He and Brandt had begun to share women in their early twenties but had never imagined they would have the opportunity to have a full relationship with one special woman between them. That was until they had arrived in Slick Rock and found that their cousins Giles, Remy, and Brandon were in the process of wooing the woman they wanted to share.

Kayli had accepted their overtures, and eventually she had let them into her bed and finally her heart. Now all three brothers worked from home and helped Kayli look after their baby, while Cord and Brandt held things down at the office.

They had been in the small Colorado town for nearly twelve months now and had just moved into their newly built house. Their cousins had asked them to buy into the security company after Cord and Brandt had retired from the police force.

Theirs wasn't the only polyandrous relationship in Slick Rock. As far as he knew, there were five other unconventional marriages in town. Now that they were settled in business as well as in their house, all they needed was a woman to complete them.

Was she the one they had been waiting for?

A loud crash resonated through the room when one of the waitstaff was accidently knocked by a patron and she dropped the tray of dirty dishes she had been carrying. Cord saw the woman across from them jump, and then she just seemed to disappear from her seat. She slid from the seat of the booth and slipped beneath the table, curling up into the fetal position with her arms around her head, trying to hide her face.

What the fuck? Quickly moving from his seat, he hunkered down and cautiously reached out. Placing his hand on her calf, he ran it up and down her leg in a soothing motion. He was aware of Brandt standing behind him, trying to block the scene of the woman's fear from prying eyes.

The whimpering sounds she made nearly broke his heart. This woman had obviously been to hell and back, and he wanted to haul her into his arms and offer her comfort, wrapping her tight in his embrace.

"It's okay, baby. You're safe here. No one is going to hurt you," Cord said quietly but loud enough for her to hear. Keeping up the soothing motions of his hand and nonsensical noises, he felt the tension slowly leave her body. She lifted her head slowly, her fear-glazed eyes meeting his. They were such a beautiful color, a mix of brown and gold with flecks of green, but her irises were nearly drowned out by her dilated pupils. Holding her gaze, he extended his hand to help her from beneath the table and watched as she lowered her eyes. He pushed his attraction aside, more concerned about her well-being, and her face pinkened with embarrassment when she realized where she was.

"Are you okay?" Cord asked when she wouldn't meet his eyes. She gave him a nod and finally lifted her arm and reached out for his hand. Tingling heat enveloped his hand and shot straight down to his crotch. The trembling of her fingers and palm pulled at his heart, and he wanted to get to the bottom of her fear and help her in any way he could. Her hand was so small compared to his, as well as really cold and clammy. Being as gentle as he could, he pulled her out from under the table, her ass sliding on the linoleum floor. When her head and body had cleared, he helped her to her feet. Keeping his hand around hers, he stood from his squatting position, placed his other hand on her waist, and helped her to her feet. Instead of sitting her back at her own table, he moved backward, gently guiding her to sit next to him in their booth.

"My name is Cord Alcott, and this is my brother, Brandt." He indicated with his head as Brandt sat down on the other side of her.

"Shelby," she began and then cleared her throat. "Shelby Richmond."

"Pleased to meet you, Shelby," Brandt said, and Cord saw the color rise in her face again. Even though she tried to hide her shiver, he saw that, too.

"Are you all right, Shelby?"

"Yes," she squeaked out in a high-pitched voice, and then the color drained from her face, leaving her so white Cord was scared she was about to pass out. Her breathing was escalated, and he could see the rapid beat of her pulse in the hollow at the base of her throat.

Just then the waitress brought Shelby's order and placed it on the table in front of her. She took his and Brandt's orders and left again.

Shelby picked up her iced tea and gulped half the glass, her hand still trembling slightly.

Cord knew she was far from okay but didn't want to make her any more uncomfortable than she already was.

"Do you live in Slick Rock, Shelby?" Brandt queried.

"No."

"Where are you from?" Cord asked.

"Illinois, Bloomington to be exact."

"You're quite a distance from home. What brought you here?" Brandt inquired.

"Um, I just needed a change of scenery."

Cord realized that Shelby was becoming uncomfortable again, because she was fidgeting and squirming in her seat, so he changed the subject.

"We're part owners of the local security company and have only been in town for a little over twelve months. We're retired cops and love how the pace of this town is much more relaxed than the city."

Shelby nodded, letting him know she had heard him, but kept her eyes lowered. She took deep breaths and released them slowly. This time when she reached for her glass, her hand was a lot steadier. It looked like little Shelby was back in control again. Finally she looked up and gazed to him then Brandt.

"Thank you," she said so quietly that Cord found himself leaning toward her to hear her.

"You don't have to thank us, Shelby, we didn't do anything," Brandt replied.

"Yes, you did. You kept prying eyes away from me."

"We would have done the same for anyone, baby," Cord stated. "Do you want to talk about it?"

"No."

"So, how do you like Slick Rock, darlin'?" Brandt inquired.

"I–It's fine. But I'm not staying."

Cord looked over to Brandt and knew his brother was thinking the same as him. Little Shelby was running from something. He wanted to pick her up, carry her out to the truck, and take her home, where they could keep an eye on her and make sure she was safe. When he realized where his thoughts were at, he knew that this woman was worth courting.

Shelby was pushing the salad in front of her with her fork, but she didn't look to be interested in eating. Cord sighed when the waitress brought their order. He began to eat, hoping she would settle enough to do the same.

"How long will you be stayin', little one?" Brandt queried.

Cord held his breath while he waited for Shelby to answer. He didn't want to hear that she would be moving on. Exhaling slowly, he watched her expectantly and saw a gamut of emotions flit across her expressive face. She went from concern to fear and finally resignation and then lifted her eyes to Brandt.

"I don't know, but I need a job. You wouldn't happen to know anyone hiring, would you?"

"Maybe. What is it you're looking for?"

"Just a way to earn some cash. Enough so I can get my radiator fixed, and then I can move on."

"You having car trouble, baby?" Cord inquired. He caught himself hoping her answer would be yes. Normally he wouldn't wish car trouble on anyone, but…

"Yeah, my radiator boiled just as I hit town. I haven't even had a chance to take it to a mechanic yet, but I know that I'm going to need a new one. Probably other things as well." She sighed.

"Well, it just so happens that we know both the shops in town. One is fairly new, but I'd trust the Badons with any of my vehicles," Brandt stated.

"You have more than one car?"

"We have a truck each and take them to Quin, Grayson, and Pierson Badon whenever we need something done. If you like, we could take you over to their place after we've eaten and they'll give you the lowdown," Cord suggested.

"I don't have much of a choice," she replied on another sigh. "What about work? Do you know where I could get a job?"

Cord raised an eyebrow at Brandt and knew his brother understood his unspoken question when he gave a slight nod. Shifting his gaze back to Shelby, he noticed she had actually started to eat rather than play with her food. Hoping she was relaxing now that they were talking with her, he tried to reach out to her.

"As it happens, we have a need for a receptionist and administration assistant. We need someone to answer the phones, do the filing, and such. Do you think you may be interested?"

"Yes," she answered quickly, as if she was grabbing onto a lifeline, unwilling to let go.

"What did you do before you left home?" Brandt asked.

"I worked in sales for a telephone company."

"Well, that definitely means you have computer and phone knowledge. I think you'd be perfect for the job. What do you say, Shelby? Do you want to come and work for us?" Cord queried.

"I think I'd be stupid to turn you down," she answered. "Do you know where I could find a room to rent?"

"You can stay with us," Brandt said and quickly continued before Shelby could interrupt him. "We have a brand-new house with more room than we know what to do with. It would be nice to have other company around rather than just ourselves."

"I'm not a charity case," Shelby said belligerently, narrowing her eyes at first Brandt and then Cord with a firm stare.

"Never thought you were, little girl. Board is fifty bucks a week, meals and utilities are included," Cord stated in a firm voice. He was loathe to take her money, but he knew damn well she would balk if he didn't. Shelby was obviously a woman who was self-reliant, and she wasn't about to give up her independence for anyone.

"Tell me about the job and pay," she commanded, thrusting her chin at him as if going into battle.

Oh darlin', you are so fucking sexy. I can't wait to hold you in my arms. The idea of holding a naked Shelby in his arms was even more appealing. Pushing his lascivious thoughts aside, he began to tell her what they expected of her and what her pay would be. When he was done he let her think over her decision as she finally finished her salad and iced tea.

"Okay, I accept. Thank you."

"No, thank you. You are going to save us a lot of wasted time by answering phones and the like," Brandt said. "Are you finished, Shelby?"

"Yes."

"Then how about we get your car over to the Badons', and then we can get you settled into your room?" Cord suggested.

"Okay."

Brandt moved out of the booth first and turned back to help Shelby to her feet. Cord heard her gasp as his brother's hand enveloped hers, and he knew she was feeling the same thing he had when he had touched her. She pulled her hand back quickly as if she had been singed and followed Brandt to the door. Cord wanted to know if she was affected by his touch, too. Shelby had been too lost in her world of panic when he'd touched her previously.

He placed his hand down low on her back, just above her ass, and nearly smiled when he saw a slight shudder run the length of her spine. *Oh yeah.* She wanted him just as much. Now he and Brandt had to convince her to begin a relationship with them. But not too quickly, or they would send her running.

Chapter Two

Shelby's gaze locked onto Brandt's tight ass as she followed him out the door. She nearly jumped out of her skin when Cord placed a guiding hand on her lower back, and the heat of his flesh seeped through her clothes, making goose bumps rise up on her skin and causing her to shiver. Every time one of the men touched her, heat and electrical pulses zinged to her breasts, curled in her womb, and shot straight down to her pussy. She had never felt anything like it before and didn't know if she liked it. In fact, she was pretty sure she didn't.

After what she had been through in the past six months, the last thing she needed was to get involved in a relationship. She was a mess, and until she had her life back under control, getting involved with someone else would only create more problems. *Keep your mind from the two gorgeous men you are going to be working with and concentrate on getting well. You don't need any more complications in your life, girl.*

"Shelby, honey, are you all right?" Brandt asked, frowning with concern.

Shelby looked up and realized she was standing on the pavement staring into space. He had obviously been talking to her, and she had been so lost with her own introspection she hadn't noticed. Her cheeks heated and she lowered her eyes, trying to regain control.

"I'm fine. Sorry, I was lost in thought. What did you ask?"

"Where is your car parked, baby?"

Shelby frowned at the endearment, even though she secretly liked it. She didn't know these men and, since she would be working for them, didn't think it was appropriate.

"My name is Shelby, and my car is just around the corner." She stepped around Brandt and led the way. Her small car was parked in a parking lot behind the diner and adjacent businesses. Praying they wouldn't see the hole in the rear window, she indicated her car and pushed the lock-release button. Even though it had been nearly six months since the incident, she didn't have insurance or the money to fix the window. So she had placed tape over the hole and hoped like hell the cops didn't pull her over for an unroadworthy car. So far so good. No one had taken any notice of the small hole and cracked glass around it.

As she turned to face the two men, heat suffused her face and body once more. God, they were so hot. Brandt looked to be younger than Cord at about thirty years old. He had the blackest hair she had ever seen. The fading sun caught the strands, making them look almost blue. His eyes were deep pools of an almost aquamarine color, and he was built like a god.

She let her gaze wander the length of his body, shielding her eyes with her lowered eyelashes as she took him in. He stood just over six feet, with broad shoulders, muscular pectorals, and bulging biceps. Her eyes snagged on the ink on his right bicep, and her pussy leaked as she traced the sexy tattoo. She couldn't see it all, because it went beneath the sleeve of his tight black T-shirt, but oh, how she would have loved to trace it with the tips of her fingers. Even though he was muscular, Brandt wasn't so pumped that he looked like a bodybuilder. His waist tapered down to narrow hips and sturdy thighs.

Surreptitiously sliding her gaze to Cord, she took him in. She felt like drooling as she perused his length. He was shorter than Brandt by an inch and had dark, chocolate-colored hair with gray eyes. With wider shoulders and slightly more muscle than his brother, he portrayed an air of self-confidence which seemed to tug at her core.

Both his arms were covered in ink that ran beneath his T-shirt. His chest and stomach were thicker than Brandt's, but there wasn't an ounce of fat on him. The muscles of his abs were visible when he moved, rippling beneath the light material of his tight cotton shirt. Her pussy clenched and creamed when her eyes wandered to his strong, muscular quadriceps and then snagged at his crotch. The man was packing a lethal weapon, and it was fully loaded. Sliding her eyes back to Brandt's crotch, she saw he was in the same condition as his brother.

Drawing in a deep breath, she turned her back on them and opened the door to her car. As she eased into the driver's seat, she exhaled slowly, releasing some of the tension which had invaded her body. Shelby was about to turn the key in the ignition, but a hand over hers stayed the movement.

"What happened to the window, Shelby?" Cord asked.

Shit, I should have known they would notice. They were cops for crying out loud, and now they run a security company. They've been trained to notice small details. You are such an idiot, Shelby. You shouldn't have accepted their job offer. Now they are going to probe and question until they get answers.

Shelby didn't want to answer those questions. She didn't want to face all that fear again. She was barely hanging on as it was. Bringing the past to the forefront of her mind might be just enough to tip her over the edge.

"Stone," she lied.

Cord looked at her quizzically. As if he knew she was lying but was deciding whether to press her. She exhaled heavily when he nodded and released her hand. She looked away from him quickly.

"Brandt, you wanna go get the truck and meet us at Quin's?" Cord asked, and Shelby was grateful he was no longer watching her. She relaxed a little more into the driver's seat and turned the ignition. To her surprise, her car started without a protest.

Cord moved around the front of her car and got into the passenger seat, moving the seat back to make room for his legs. He began to direct her to his mechanic friends'. Shelby had never been more aware of a man's presence in such a confined space. She was having trouble breathing, but this time for a totally different reason than before. The atmosphere in her car felt so thick with sexual tension that she swore she could have cut it with a knife. Opening the window, she inhaled deeply the clean country air, held it for a count of three, and exhaled quietly. It was one of the tricks her psychologist had given her, but it didn't help all the time. At least not in this instance.

Finally, she was able to pull her car into the driveway of the mechanics and quickly scampered from the vehicle before Brandt could open her door. He had been heading toward her with three men in tow, but she wasn't sure how she would react if one of them were to touch her again. The radiator in her car took that opportunity to hiss and blow some steam.

"Shelby, this is Quin, Grayson, and Pierson Badon. They are going to take a look at your car," Brandt said.

After the introductions were over and Shelby made it clear to the Badon brothers they were to consult with her about her car before they touched it, Cord and Brandt began to unload her things from the backseat and trunk. It didn't take them long, since she didn't have much, but what she did have was hers, and no one was going to damage it. Especially her books. She had two cardboard boxes filled to the brim with her precious reading material, and she grieved over the ones she had had to leave behind. She was glad she had taped the lids closed.

When Brandt reached into the backseat and removed her quilt and pillow, she caught him looking at Cord. It seemed almost like the brothers could communicate without opening their mouths. Just a twitch of a brow and a responsive nod let her know her speculation was correct. God, she so missed the closeness of having a loving family. Tears filled her eyes, and she swallowed audibly around the lump in her throat. Quickly looking away from the two brothers, she reached into her car for her purse.

"Are you okay, little one?" Cord's voice and heated breath brushed against her ear as she straightened, and he wrapped his arms around her waist.

Oh God. Don't touch me. Don't be nice to me. If you do, I'm scared I'll break.

"Fine," she replied coldly. "Back off."

Cord released her instantly, and the heat at her back was replaced by the cooling evening air. She turned around but didn't look at Cord, and then she handed her car keys over to Quin.

"Are you all right, sugar?" Quin asked.

Shelby narrowed her eyes at him and saw his brothers were watching her just as intently. They looked concerned. "I'm fine."

"If you ever need anything, Shelby, all you have to do is call," Grayson stated, taking her hand in his and giving her a reassuring squeeze.

"Thanks," she answered.

"Shelby has us. She doesn't need to call you," Brandt snapped in a steely voice. He slipped an arm through hers, gently pulling her away from Grayson.

Oh for goodness' sake, are they going to have a pissing contest?

Pulling away from Brandt, she glared at him. Didn't the man realize his friend wasn't coming on to her, he was just offering her a bit of human compassion?

"Brandt, we need to get home so Shelby can get settled," Cord said and took her hand, leading her to the truck.

He opened the passenger door for her, and she eyed the big step and the seat. She would have had a bit of a struggle to get in, but she wasn't given the chance to try. Large, warm hands gripped her waist and lifted her. She squeaked, but then she turned her head, her gaze connecting with Cord's.

"Don't argue. I was just helping," Cord said firmly and closed the back door.

Shelby released an agitated breath. *God, how am I going to survive living and working with these men? I'm already a bundle of nerves, and the more I'm with them the more I want them.*

Pulling on her seat belt, she stared out the window as the two Alcott brothers got into the truck. She shored up her defenses and vowed she would work long enough to pay for her car plus a little spending money and then she would leave without a backward glance. Her sanity and body wouldn't endure much more.

* * * *

Brandt spent the drive home berating himself for his jealousy. He hadn't known how possessive he felt toward Shelby until Grayson had offered to help her if she needed it. Shelby had been pissed at his reaction, and rightly so. So was Cord, but no more than Brandt was mad at himself.

When he had seen the bullet hole in her rear window and pointed it out to Cord, he felt first anger and then fear that she had been in danger. He believed Shelby had lied to his brother when asked about the bullet hole, and he had wanted to haul her up into his arms to reassure her she was safe with them.

She was such a sexy little thing, and even though she tried to hide it, her body language as well as her scent of aroused woman let him know she wasn't immune to him or Cord. But until she was more comfortable, he wouldn't push her. He didn't want her leaving before they had a chance to get to know her, because he knew deep down in his heart and soul that he could very easily fall in love with her.

Pulling into the drive, he parked the truck near the verandah so they could unload Shelby's things. With a sigh he turned off the ignition and walked around to the other side of the vehicle. Cord's hands on her tiny waist as he helped her down from the truck looked so right, and his cock twitched. She kept her eyes down and wouldn't look at him, so he waited until his brother stepped back and then Brandt gently tilted her face up.

"I'm sorry, Shelby. I don't know what came over me. I'm not normally like that."

Shelby stood studying him intently, and he held her gaze. She must have seen his sincerity, because she gave him a tentative smile and a nod. Brandt exhaled, releasing her, and turned to the bed of the truck for her things. It didn't take him and Cord long to unload, and when they had her things stored in her room, he showed her around the house. Once that was done, he and Cord left her to unpack and headed to the kitchen.

"What the hell, Brandt. You nearly blew it before we've even started!" Cord exclaimed.

"I know. I apologized."

"You're going to have to back off, or you'll scare her."

"You think I don't know that? Fuck, Cord, I didn't even know I was going to go all He-Man." Brandt reached for the coffeepot and set about making fresh coffee.

"What do you think happened to her back window?"

"Other than being shot at, your guess is as good as mine."

"That girl is in a shitload of trouble."

"Yeah, but how are we going to protect her if she doesn't open up to us?"

Chapter Three

Shutting down her PC and making sure everything was tidy, Shelby double-checked the filing cabinets were locked as well as the filing room. In the past week, Shelby became accustomed to living and working with the two Alcott brothers. She found her job interesting and fulfilling, and she was relieved not to be on the road for the first time in what seemed like forever.

But she was still haunted by her nightmares. She was just thankful that so far she hadn't screamed and woken her two housemates in the middle of the night. Often she would awaken with her heart pounding in her chest, her body covered in sweat and shaking after reliving the incident.

It was very rare that she was able to relax enough to go back to sleep. Thank God she had brought some of her beloved books with her. She spent the hours until she had to get up reading, but she was so tired she didn't know how much more sleep deprivation she could stand.

Just as she returned to her desk, Brandt and Cord stepped out of their office. Brandt and Cord spent a lot of time in there, sending out private investigators to follow up leads for their clients. They checked out everything from companies to spouses, confirming or denying their clients' suspicions of infidelity or illegitimacy, corporate espionage or embezzlement, all from their desks.

"Are you ready, Shelby?" asked Cord.

"Yes, I'm done."

"Good, let's go and get cleaned up so we aren't late," Brandt advised and took her elbow, leading her out.

Tonight they had been invited to a barbecue over at Brandt and Cord's cousins' house, and even though Shelby was looking forward to meeting new people and a change of scenery, she was nervous. The Alcott brothers had told her of the polyamorous relationships in the town, and even though she had no problem with how others lived their lives, she was scared she would say or do something untoward.

When they got back home, Shelby went straight to the kitchen. "Why don't you two go and shower while I make coffee and finish up the potato salad?"

"Okay. Just holler if you want help with something," Cord replied, and then he and Brandt headed down the hall.

Shelby put the finishing touches on the potato salad. Once that was done, she poured herself a coffee and sat at the table to sip it. She was only vaguely aware of Cord entering the kitchen again, since she was lost in thought, but when he dropped the mug on the tile floor and it exploded into little pieces, she was transported back to that horrible day.

* * * *

A loud explosion startled her. She was following her mother into the living room after a wonderful meal shared with her parents and her brother, Ian. Her mom was carrying the coffee into the living room. Her father had just risen to his feet to take the tray from her mom, but he never reached them.

Glass exploded all around them, but Shelby couldn't move. She watched with frozen horror as first her dad, then her mom crumpled to the floor.

"Get down!" Ian screamed. Shelby only stared at him as she slowly realized that her parents' house was being peppered with gunfire from outside. Ian crawled toward her on the floor, dragged her down, and shoved her behind the sofa. Whimpering with fear, Shelby looked around the room for her parents.

Her mom and dad were covered in blood and stared out of unseeing eyes. Ian crawled on the floor over to her parents with a cell phone clamped to his ear. She could see his mouth moving but couldn't hear any sound. With tears streaming down his face, he checked her parents' pulse points, but Shelby knew already that it was too late. Keeping her eyes connected with her brother's, she reached out toward him, beckoning, needing him close in a world gone so mad that she couldn't comprehend anything.

Ian inched toward her, crawling along the floor on his belly. He was covered with blood, and even though she was in shock, she knew it wasn't his. Just as his hand connected with hers, he jerked. Shelby peered from behind the sofa. The evil face stared at her from the smashed window. He kept his gaze focused on her and pulled the trigger. Ian squeezed her hand one last time and then let go. The face in the window was gone. A car engine revved in the street. She was alone.

Shelby screamed and screamed and screamed.

* * * *

The mug Cord had been holding smashed on the tiles, almost drowning out the whimper of fear that came at the same moment. Turning toward Shelby, he rushed to her side as she slipped beneath the table. He pulled her into his arms and rocked her, but she was lost in a nightmare. She reached out, but he didn't know for what, and then she was screaming. The sound was so tortured, so full of animalistic pain and grief, that it tore at his heart.

Brandt came running, bare chested with his jeans barely on, and slid to a halt when he saw Shelby in his arms. He moved behind her and smoothed a hand up and down her back. They were both calling her name.

"Shelby, you're safe, baby," Cord crooned over and over

"Darlin', it's going to be okay," Brandt said quietly.

Cord knew the instant Shelby came out of her nightmare. She stiffened in his arms, gave one last sob, and then slumped down against him, her fingers locked in the fabric of his shirt. He was strong enough that there was no danger of dropping her. Cord stood with ease, cradling her in his arms and sitting down on a chair. Shelby continued to clutch at him, and her body spasmed with the occasional hiccup.

"Shh, little one. You're safe here. We won't let anything happen to you," Cord whispered against her ear.

He felt her muscles tauten as she gathered up her defenses, then she eased her head off his chest and sat up.

"I'm sorry," she said in a tear-husky voice.

Brandt squatted down next to them and ran his hand up and down her thigh. "You have absolutely nothing to be sorry for, darlin'."

"Look at me, Shelby," Cord commanded softly and waited for her to comply. When she looked up at him, his heart clenched, and he had to swallow the lump of emotion in his throat before he could continue. "You don't need to apologize, baby. I'm the one who's sorry. I didn't mean to scare you."

"You didn't. It's me," she replied.

"No, Shelby, it's not you. Do you want to talk about it?"

"No. I can't. It's too painful."

"We're here when you're ready, darlin'. Do you still feel up to going out?" Brandt queried.

"Shit. I forgot," she said and pushed off Cord. "I'll be ready to go in about ten minutes."

Cord watched her scurry from the room on unsteady legs. He wanted to go with her but knew she wouldn't allow any help.

"Fuck, Cord. What the hell happened to her?" Brandt asked with frustration, running his hand over his face.

"I don't know. But I intend to find out. She can't keep going on like this. She's going to end up sick and in the hospital. Did you see the dark smudges beneath her eyes?"

"Yeah. I hear her pacing the floor in the early hours, and her light's on more often than not. We have to get her to talk, or she's going to snap."

"I know. Maybe we can enlist Kayli's help," Cord suggested. "She probably knows more than anyone what Shelby's feeling."

"That's not a bad idea. Go and call Giles and let him know we want Kayli to talk to Shelby tonight. Maybe the compassion of another woman will get her to open up."

* * * *

As soon as Shelby met Kayli, she knew they would become friends. The woman was gorgeous and so full of love and life that she felt a pang of envy. Her husbands, Giles, Remy and Brandon, were handsome, and they treated their wife like a queen. Sipping her glass of wine, Shelby listened to the men's witty repartee and couldn't help laughing along with them. The meal had been delicious, and she couldn't remember feeling so drained of energy. She stifled a yawn and tried to hide how exhausted she felt.

"Shelby, can you give me a hand with dessert?" Kayli asked with a smile.

"Sure," she replied, rising to her feet and following into the house from the verandah, where the alfresco dining had been set up.

They chatted easily, as if they had known each other for years, as they worked together.

"You look tired. Are you okay?" Kayli asked.

"Yeah."

"If you ever want to talk, just call me."

Shelby swallowed around the lump in her throat and lowered her head to hide the tears forming in her eyes. "Thanks."

"Did Cord and Brandt tell you how I came to Slick Rock?"

"No."

Kayli went on and told her how she had witnessed murder in a bank holdup and how she had run when the perpetrators had found out where she lived. She went on to explain how those "motherfuckers" had tracked her down and nearly killed her.

Tears streamed down Shelby's cheeks, and she felt the color drain from her face. Kayli's story was so close to her own, except that the murders Shelby had witnessed were far more personal.

Shelby blanched when Kayli wrapped her arms around her, but then she clung to the other woman and cried. She sobbed until she could hardly breathe and saw herself as if from a long way off, standing over her own body looking down. She heard herself telling Kayli how her family had been wiped out in a mad rampage of violence. How the perpetrator was now incarcerated and she'd testified against him at trial. How the memories were making her crazy and she was running. Shelby wanted to be as far away from her hometown as possible.

But no matter where she ran to she couldn't escape the nightmares.

How long they sat on the floor with her clinging to Kayli, Shelby had no idea, and if it hadn't been for Kayli's baby waking up from a nap and crying out, she may have clung to the poor woman all night.

The back door clicking shut and then a masculine voice crooning to the infant penetrated her grief-stricken haze. It was only when she heard the men outside talking to the baby that she realized the windows were open and the men probably heard every word she had spoken.

"Oh God," she sobbed, easing away from Kayli. "I'm so sorry."

"Don't you dare apologize," Kayli said. "You have nothing to be sorry for. Do you want another drink? Even though I'm not supposed to, I could use one right about now."

Kayli got up from the floor and pulled a bottle of whiskey and two glasses from the cupboard. She poured two shots, handed one to Shelby, and smiled. "Bottoms up."

Shelby downed the drink in one swallow and coughed as it burned down her esophagus and into her stomach. When she was done, Kayli handed her the other glass and laughed as she downed that one, too.

"Come on, let's go and enjoy dessert." Kayli beckoned.

On unsteady legs, Shelby helped take out the apple pies and ice cream and sat down again. The men were all cooing and laughing at the baby.

"She's so small," Shelby slurred and giggled.

"Do you want to hold her?" Kayli asked.

"I don't think that's such a good idea." She giggled again. Covering her mouth, she looked sheepishly at Brandt and Cord. They were smiling at her, but she could also see concern and desire in their eyes. Shivering as the night air cooled, she looked away quickly.

"Are you cold, baby?" Cord asked, his warm breath caressing her ear.

"A little."

"Come here, then, and let me warm you."

Shelby eyed him quizzically as Cord scooted his chair back and reached for her. He lifted her from her chair with ease and placed her on his lap. His arms wrapped around her, and the heat radiating from his large, muscular body began to seep into her.

"You're hot," she stated.

"Why thank you, baby, you're sexy, too," he said and looked down at her with a smile.

Shelby giggled and shifted on his lap. "That's not what I meant, but you're that, too."

"I think it's time we took you home, darlin'," Brandt said. "You're drunk."

"I am not. I never get ine–ineb…drunk."

Cord stood up, taking her with him, and she smiled when Kayli laughed.

"Thank you for a lov–lovel…nice dinner."

"You're welcome. Call me, Shelby. We can go shopping together."

"Okay," she said on a sigh and snuggled into Cord's warmth. Inhaling deeply, she took in his clean, masculine scent. "You smell nice."

"You do, too, baby," he replied as he carried her.

"Do you know how handsome you are?" she asked with a giggle. "You and Brandt are *sooo* sexy."

"It's definitely time you were in bed, little girl."

"Hmm, sleepy."

Even through her drowsiness, though, she was pricked by an uneasy sensation. Had the men heard everything she'd said to Kayli? She didn't want them to know all that, not yet. They'd never want anything to do with her if they knew about her nightmares. It was bad enough for them to have seen her freak out in the kitchen earlier.

She didn't want to think about it now. She just wanted a moment to enjoy the feeling of being carried and supported.

"Close your eyes, baby. You're safe with us," Cord stated, and Shelby knew that she was, no matter what came next. She closed her eyes, snuggled in, and slept.

Chapter Four

Brandt sighed with relief when they were finally in the truck heading home. He glanced in the rearview mirror. "How is she?"

"Asleep," Cord replied.

"Thank God."

"Yeah."

They'd heard Shelby purge her grief to Kayli. Brandt's heart still ached so bad that he rubbed his chest. He'd wanted to go inside and take Shelby into his arms and soothe her, but he knew he couldn't do anything to take her pain away. So he'd sat in his chair, gripping the armrests until his hands ached. The tortured sounds coming out of her mouth still rang in his ears. He was reminded of the cries of a wounded animal.

Thank God for Kayli. If she hadn't told her story, Brandt didn't know if Shelby would have opened up to anyone.

Brandt pulled the truck into the garage and switched off the engine. Getting out, he opened the back door and took Shelby into his arms.

"She feels so right, Cord," he whispered.

"I know."

Brandt carried Shelby into the house and to her room. He placed her on the bed and removed her shoes. "Do you think we should make her more comfortable?"

"No. We don't want to betray her trust," Cord replied. "Pick her up, and I'll pull the covers back."

When they had her in bed, Brandt sat on the edge and smoothed her hair back from her face. Looking up to his brother, he saw the same anguish he felt mirrored back at him. Fury at the senseless violence done to Shelby and her family made him feel sick to his stomach.

He tried to focus on the woman in front of him to control his anger and sorrow. "She's so fucking gorgeous. I'm half in love with her already."

"Me, too."

"Do you think she'll be all right?"

"I don't know." Cord sighed.

The question now was when she'd feel ready to tell them. It was hard to tell from Shelby's tipsy behavior, but he didn't think she knew that they'd overheard everything. Even if she did, Brandt reflected, he wanted to hear it from her own lips. It would be a sign that she trusted them and was ready to move on.

"Leave the door open. That way, if she wakes up, we'll hear her."

Brandt looked back over his shoulder at the sleeping woman and slipped out of the room. He followed Cord to the kitchen.

"I want her, Cord."

"I do, too."

"Do you think it's too soon?" he asked.

"I don't know, Brandt. Shit, she's been through hell and is suffering from Post-Traumatic Stress Disorder."

"She said we were sexy," Brandt said with a smile.

"Yeah, I know, but that doesn't mean she wants a relationship with us."

"I want to find out," Brandt stated. "She looks at you when she thinks no one's watching, and I can see such hunger in her eyes."

"She looks at you the same."

"She does?"

"Yeah."

"Well, I think we should start wooing her. I don't want her leaving. I want her here with us, in our arms and bed, where we can keep her safe."

"Wait and see how she feels. Maybe now she talked out her grief, she'll be ready."

* * * *

"Wake up, darlin'," Brandt coaxed, rubbing a hand up and down Shelby's arm.

He smiled when she sighed and stretched. She looked like a little kitten just waking up from a nap.

"Hmm?"

"I have coffee." Brandt ran the mug back and forth beneath her nose. Her eyes opened fully. "There you are. Did you sleep well?"

"Yes," she replied, and Brandt heard the surprise in her voice.

"Glad to hear it, darlin'." He handed her the mug. "Do you want to go for a horse ride today?"

"I've never been on a horse."

"That doesn't matter. I'm sure we can find you a quiet horse. Tom and Billy Eagle, Sheriff Luke Sun-Walker, and their wife, Felicity, have invited us out to the Double E Ranch for a ride. Their friends Clay and Johnny Morten and their wife, Tara, will also be there."

"That sounds nice," she answered with a smile. "What time do you want to leave?"

"As soon as you're ready, darlin'."

"Then you'd better get out of here so I can move."

"Okay, but there's no need to hurry, Shelby." He gave her a smile as he left the room.

"Does she want to come?" Cord asked Brandt when he returned to the kitchen. "Shit, get that look off your face, that's not what I meant and you know it."

"Sorry," Brandt replied with a waggle of his eyebrows. "Yes, she looked excited."

"Good. That girl needs some fun in her life," Cord said and took his mug to the table.

Brandt sat with his brother in companionable silence as they waited for Shelby. When he heard her footsteps in the hall, his cock twitched and he looked toward the door. Biting his tongue so he wouldn't moan out loud, he took in the jeans molded to her hips and shapely thighs and then perused his way up her shirt, which clung to her breasts. Her face was a shiny pink, and she looked like a sex goddess.

"I'm ready. Did you need to bring anything?" Shelby asked.

"No, darlin', just ourselves," Brandt answered. "Do you have a hat? I don't want you getting sunburned."

"No."

"We'll ask Felicity if she has a spare. Come on, let's head on out." Cord took Shelby's hand.

* * * *

Shelby couldn't believe how happy the members of Slick Rock's polyamorous relationships were. The men were attentive to their wives' needs, and the women seemed to glow from all the affection. She watched the love-filled interaction between spouses as she rode her gentle horse and couldn't help but feel slightly envious. What would it be like to have the love and attention of more than one husband?

"How are you doing, baby?" Cord asked. He was riding a large horse on one side, and Brandt was on her other. She appreciated that they kept close to her since she'd never ridden before.

"Good. This is so much fun. It's such a beautiful day." All the tension she had carried around with her seemed to have fallen away after her crying jag last night, and she didn't even feel hungover. Shelby felt as if she wasn't drowning for the first time in months.

"How long are you planning on staying in Slick Rock, Shelby?" Felicity called out.

"I don't know. I haven't made any fast plans." If she was honest with herself, she didn't have any plans at all except to keep running.

At the same time, she hadn't even thought about her car in days. Shelby frowned. It had to be fixed by now, didn't it?

Tara's voice drew her back to the conversation.

"Do you like our little town, Shelby?" Tara queried.

"Yes. It's so clean and peaceful. I can see myself staying here." She sighed wistfully at the thought of a future here.

But she wasn't sure if she could have that. Brandt and Cord knew what had happened now, or at least she thought they had overheard her telling Kayli last night. The idea made her feel self-conscious. The men had seemed interested in her last night, and they were certainly attentive this morning, but there was no way they'd stay interested now that they knew what a wreck she was.

Yet as soon as the thought crossed her mind, Brandt said, "We want you to stay, too, darlin'." He reached over to stroke her thigh.

Shelby felt her cheeks heat as Brandt's touch sent zings of tingling warmth shooting through her blood and pooling in her pussy. Another touch to her arm from her other side drew her attention, and she looked into Cord's heated gaze.

"I love that you are living and working with us, baby. The house would feel so empty without you."

Looking away as more heat suffused her cheeks, Shelby shifted in the saddle, trying to ease the ache in her pussy. God, they were so handsome and sexy, she wanted to jump their bones. Every time she turned around one or the other of them was looking at her with desire, but neither one of them had made a move on her. *They say they want me to stay.* But did that mean they wanted her to stay with them? Maybe after they heard her meltdown, they'd decided she wasn't worth the effort. Sighing with resignation, she pushed her thoughts aside, intending to enjoy the summer day.

After they were back at the house and had enjoyed another barbecue, Felicity suggested they take a swim in the pool. Shelby looked at the clear water with longing but shook her head, since she hadn't brought any swimwear with her.

"I have a couple of bathing suits, Shelby. Come and try them on," Felicity said enticingly.

The day had become quite hot, and Shelby wanted nothing more than to dive into the cool water, so she let Felicity lead her into the house, Tara walking behind her.

The women giggled as they took out their suits, and Shelby was thankful when Tara handed her a two-piece bathing suit. "I always bring more than one, just in case."

"Thanks," Shelby replied, taking the suit and stepped into the bathroom. Studying herself in the mirror, she twisted around, looking at her body from all angles. Even though she and Tara were practically the same height, Shelby's hips were wider and her bust smaller. The bikini looked nearly indecent on her body. She just wished Felicity's one-piece had fit her. Then she wouldn't be so self-conscious when she went outside wearing bits of nothing.

"Come on out, Shelby," Tara called. "You can't hide in there all afternoon."

Taking a deep breath, Shelby finally opened the door.

"Oh, girl, you look so sexy. Those two men are going to fall at your feet," Tara stated with a smile.

"I don't think this is such a good idea."

"Shelby, you look stunning. If I had a figure like yours, I'd go around naked," Felicity said.

"What are you talking about, girl?" Tara asked with a frown. "You're sex on legs. Why is it that we women are never happy with what we have? We shouldn't question what God gave us, and since our men adore our bodies, who cares if we're not perfect."

"She's right, you know," Felicity said. "And if the looks those two Alcott brothers give you are an indication, you are doomed, girl."

"Do you think so?" Shelby asked uncertainly.

"Oh yeah," Tara said with a giggle. "You just watch them when you go outside. I'll bet they get hard in an instant."

"Tara! You are so naughty." Felicity chuckled.

"Don't I know it, and my men love it!"

"How do you…" Shelby began then clamped her lips shut.

"How do we what?" Tara asked then smiled wickedly. "How do we have sex with more than one man? How do we put up with them? Don't be shy now, Shelby, you can ask us anything."

Shelby felt her face burn but looked at both women. "How does sex with more than one man feel? Sorry, don't answer that. The question is too personal."

"Out of this world," Tara replied seriously. "Just imagine having three, or in your case two, sets of hands running over your body. Two mouths pleasuring you and two cocks loving you. Nothing can describe how it feels to make love with men you love and who love you in return."

"Oh yeah," Felicity said with a smile.

"Oh God," Shelby moaned and shifted from foot to foot. She could just imagine one of them kissing her while the other sucked on her nipples. That image was quickly replaced with another. This time Cord had his head between her legs while Brandt suckled at her breast, and both of them would caress every inch of her body with their hands. *Shit, girl, you have it bad, but you don't even know if you're going to stay.*

"Now you've done it," Felicity said. "The girl was already horny, now she's creaming her panties."

"And you think I'm bad." Tara laughed and looked to Shelby.

Shelby gasped for air as she felt the blood drain from her face. *What the hell am I going to do?*

"Shit. You didn't realize, did you?" Felicity took one of her hands and squeezed.

"What?"

"That you're in love with them." Tara clasped her other hand. "Take a deep breath, girl, and let's go have some fun."

Chapter Five

Cord glanced up as the women stepped outside and felt all the blood in his body shoot down to his cock. He was thankful that at that particular moment he was already in the pool and nobody could see the hard-on in his cutoffs. He heard his brother groan and knew Brandt was in the same predicament.

Shelby was all woman. The suit she had borrowed looked like it had been made for her. The small triangles of material lovingly cupped her lush breasts, and the strings tied at her curvy hips tempted a man to tug them off. Her waist was so tiny he wanted to see if he could span it with his hands, and even though she wasn't tall, her thighs and calves were shapely and slim. His eyes were drawn to her hips again, and he imagined gripping them between his hands as he fucked her from behind.

"Fuck!" Brandt groaned and sunk under the water. Cord wanted to follow him so he could get his unruly cock to behave, but he couldn't take his eyes from her. She glanced toward him shyly from beneath her lashes, looking innocently sexy. He couldn't stand not having her near him.

"Come on in, baby. The water's great," he said as he swam toward the side of the pool, holding a hand out toward her.

"Is it cold?" She walked closer.

Cord was mesmerized by the sway of her hips and the slight jiggle of her breasts as she moved. His balls were aching, and he was in danger of shooting off. Clenching his other hand into a fist, he smiled and hoped she couldn't tell how much she turned him on.

"Only when you first get in." He beckoned by straightening and then curling a finger.

Shelby took a deep breath and jumped. She didn't squeal like Tara and Felicity before they hit the water. Cord made sure he was close when she surfaced and watched as she pushed her wet hair back from her face.

"It's nice."

"How about a game of water polo?" Tom Morten asked, holding up a ball.

The men cheered and laughed lasciviously, and Shelby wondered what she had gotten herself into. Johnny decided on three teams, family against family with Cord, Brandt, and Shelby as a team.

The game was fun. Cord watched as Shelby yelled and laughed along with everyone else as Felicity tried to score a goal in the small portable nets floating on the water's surface at each end of the pool.

Brandt got hold of the ball. Shelby was safe and close to the other goal, so she called for him to throw it to her. Just as the ball came hurtling toward her, Luke Sun-Walker swam toward her at a fast pace, and Cord knew she wouldn't be able to reach it before he did. All the men had an unfair advantage of height over the women. Cord grasped Shelby around the waist and lifted her high above the water. She reached up over Luke's head, plucked the ball from the air, and, with his help, turned toward the goal, threw the ball, and scored.

"You did it, baby," Cord yelled happily as he lowered her back down his body and turned her to face him. Everything and everyone around him faded away. In that moment only he and Shelby existed. He looked into her brown-gold-green-flecked eyes and felt himself drowning. Her body brushed against his, and he wrapped his arms around her waist and lowered his head. Shelby's eyes widened just before they closed and their mouths connected.

Slanting his mouth over hers, he eased her into the kiss, slowly deepening it as she responded. When she wrapped her arms around his neck and whimpered, Cord knew he had to stop. Slowing the kiss, he finally withdrew his mouth from hers and groaned with satisfaction when her passion-glazed eyes connected with his.

"If you've finished celebrating your goal, we have drinks ready," Felicity called.

Cord looked about and realized everyone else besides him, Shelby, and Brandt was already out of the pool.

"Oh God," Shelby gasped.

"Do you need some help, darlin'?" Brandt asked when Shelby swam over to the steps.

"No, I'm fine."

"You certainly are."

Cord heard Shelby draw in breath, but she didn't reply. He and Brandt swam a few laps before they got out of the pool, and the other men gave those knowing smiles and winks. Cord flopped down onto the chair next to Shelby.

"Are you having fun, baby?"

"Yes. I can't remember the last time I laughed so much. Thank you." She touched his arm.

Cord took her hand and lifted it to his lips. He smiled when her pupils dilated and her breath hitched. "You're welcome. You should laugh more often, Shelby. I like to see you happy."

"So do I," Brandt said as he sat at her other side.

They spent the rest of the afternoon chatting, but Cord noticed when Shelby began to yawn. He didn't like it that she still had dark smudges under her eyes, testimony that she hadn't been sleeping well for a long time.

"Are you ready to go home, baby?" he asked after he had changed back into his jeans and shirt.

"Yes, just let me go change and I'll be with you," she replied.

After saying their thank-yous and good-byes, they headed toward home. Shelby was asleep before they got off the Double E Ranch.

"Come on, little girl, let's get you inside," Cord said and scooped Shelby from the backseat of the truck.

"We are? Are you carrying me?" she asked drowsily.

"Yep. You feel good in my arms, Shelby. I could carry you around all day long."

"Hmm, that's nice." She snuggled into him, rubbing her cheek on his chest with her arms wrapped around his neck.

"I want you, baby," Cord stated, his need for her making his voice deep and husky.

"You do?"

"Oh yeah. You're such a sexy little thing. I want to kiss and lick you all over."

"What?" Shelby asked and stiffened in his arms. She lifted her head and stared up at him.

"I want to make love with you, Shelby. So does Brandt," Cord declared.

"Oh God," Shelby moaned.

"Will you let us, darlin'?" Brandt asked from just behind Cord.

"I–I…shit."

"Think about it, Shelby. I know you're attracted to us, too. I can smell your little creaming pussy," Cord rasped. "Just imagine what it would be like to have us touch you at the same time. It'll be so good, baby."

"But I've never had two men before. I'd never thought it possible until I heard of the other polyandrous relationships in Slick Rock."

Cord carried Shelby to her room and slid her down his aching body. He made sure she knew of his arousal, thrusting his hips into hers before her knees connected with the mattress.

"Do you trust me—us, Shelby?"

"Yes."

"And you know we'd never hurt you, right?"

"Yes."

"And you want us, don't you, baby?"

"Yes." She whispered her reply.

"Then will you let us make you feel good? Will you let us make love with you?"

"Oh God. Yes!"

That was all Cord had been waiting for. He stared deeply into her eyes and watched as her breathing escalated and desire tinged her cheeks a pink hue. Finally, when he couldn't stand it anymore, he pulled her close, bent down, and took her mouth.

She opened to him as soon as his lips connected with hers, and she sighed into his mouth. Slanting his mouth over hers, he slid his tongue into her and tasted. Shelby tasted like no other woman before her. She was pure ambrosia, and one taste would never be enough. The little whimpering sounds she made had him burning for more, and she gripped his shirt like she would never let go.

Again and again he took her, exploring every bit of her moist cavern until they were both breathless. Easing back, he kissed and nibbled his way down her neck until he reached the collar of her shirt. Lifting his head, he watched her carefully as he undid the buttons and parted the material.

"You are so fucking sexy, baby. You have no idea how much I've craved to feel you under my hands, my mouth, and my body." Shelby didn't reply, but she was panting heavily. Her eyelids were lowered, and the green in her eyes seemed to glow with her desire. Her lips were swollen and red from his kisses.

Brandt moved up beside him, and Cord reluctantly stepped back to allow his brother a taste of their woman. "Hey, darlin', are you sure about this? Because once we start there's no going back. You'll be ours, and I'm not just talking about tonight. I mean permanently. Do you understand?"

"Yes," Shelby moaned, reaching for Brandt.

Brandt kissing his woman was one of the most erotic things Cord had ever seen. He couldn't wait until they had her naked and writhing beneath them. Being careful not to interrupt his brother's moment with Shelby, he knelt on the bed behind her and pushed her shirt from her shoulders and off her arms. He measured her tiny waist with his hands. He was right, his fingers met at the front and his thumbs in her back. After pushing her hair away from her nape, he kissed and licked down her neck and across the smooth, creamy skin of her shoulders.

Cord caressed his hands over her belly and slowly inched his way up her torso, over her ribs, until he was cupping her lush breasts. He groaned when her hard little nipples stabbed into his hand. With deft fingers he flicked the front catch of her bra open and inhaled sharply when her voluptuous mounds spilled into his palms.

She whimpered into Brandt's mouth and arched into his touch as he took her hard nipples between fingers and thumbs and squeezed. Fire raced through his blood, making his cock ache and jerk against his zipper and the cum in his balls roil. Covering her with his large hands, he kneaded and caressed, exploring every inch of her soft, fleshy globes. Her body heated with need, and Cord could smell the sexy scent of her musky arousal. His mouth watered as the urge to taste her became too much to ignore. With slow deliberation, he released her breasts and caressed his way down her ribs, torso, and belly, until his fingers connected with the waistband of her jeans.

With unerring dexterity, Cord popped the button of her jeans, lowered the zipper, and hooked his fingers into the sides of the denim material, pushing the pants and her underwear over her rounded hips and down her thighs. Brushing his fingers through the soft hair of her mound, he slid his hand down until he was cupping her pussy with his fingers and the palm of his hand. Then, with slow deliberation, he began using the heel of his hand to massage her soft flesh. Shelby gasped for air as she drew away from Brandt's mouth, and her eyes closed when Cord applied rhythmic pressure to her clit, still hidden beneath the soft folds of her pussy.

Brandt bent down, removed Shelby's shoes, and pulled her jeans and panties off over her feet and ankles. Cord supported her weight by tightening his free arm around her waist, bringing her back into contact with his chest.

"She likes what you're doing to her, Cord. I can see her little pussy creaming. Shelby's so horny her thighs are wet with her juices."

"Do you like what I'm doing, baby?" Cord rumbled out.

"Yes," Shelby gasped.

"Do you want more? Do you want my fingers playing with your hard little clit and then buried in your wet cunt? Or do you want my mouth on that hot, dripping pussy?"

"Oh please!"

"What do you want, darlin'? We can't give you what you need unless you tell us what it is you want," Brandt rasped.

"Everything. Please? I want everything you said," she moaned.

"Good girl," Cord praised her, "but next time I want you to ask specifically for what you want. Do you understand, baby?"

"Yes."

Cord moved to Shelby's side and lowered her to the bed, making sure to place her in the middle of the mattress so Brandt had room to get close on her other side. He then lay down beside her and began to run a hand up and down her body, tracing all her curves and dips, making sure to take note of every erogenous zone he found. Brandt was lying on her other side, his hand caressing her, too. Between the two of them they had her twisting, writhing, and arching into their touch within moments.

"Just look at how hard those little nipples are," Brandt said in a breathless voice. "I can't wait to taste those little berries."

"I want to eat her cream." With a growl, Cord moved between Shelby's thighs.

Chapter Six

Burning. That was the only word which came to mind to describe how she felt. Shelby gasped and moaned at the way the Alcott brothers' dirty talk ratcheted her libido up another notch. She had never been so turned on in her life. Juices were leaking out of her pussy, down between the cheeks of her ass, making her asshole wet. When she'd been standing, cream had coated her thighs, and they still felt sticky. Her body felt as if it was burning from the inside out, and she knew only these two men could put out the flames.

Crying out with pleasure as two mouths simultaneously connected with her flesh, she writhed and moaned as Brandt took one of her nipples into the warm, wet heat of his mouth. Then she nearly screamed when Cord nudged her thighs apart and licked her slit from top to bottom.

This was what she had been waiting for. It was the image of the fantasy she'd had earlier that day. But it wasn't just about the sex and physical attraction. She had a deep-seated need to be near them as much as possible. They were slowly working their way into her heart, and she wasn't sure if she liked it. Maybe by making love with them she could get them out of her system and move on. Even as that thought coalesced, Shelby knew she was lying to herself. Pushing her thoughts aside for now, she concentrated on just feeling.

Brandt released her nipple from his mouth with a pop. "Easy, darlin'. We'll get you there. There's no rush, Shelby."

"You. Don't. Know…" She panted.

"What don't we know, baby?" Cord asked after lifting his head away from her pussy.

"I've never…" She halted, still breathing heavily as she sought the words she needed to make a coherent sentence.

"Never what? Never had sex? Are you a…?" Brandt began.

"No! I've just never–never…had an orgasm," Shelby finally managed to say, albeit in a rush.

"You've never come? Ever?" Cord queried.

"Of course I have," Shelby replied, "just not with a man."

"Are you trying to tell us you're bisexual, baby?"

"No!" Shelby yelled. "Oh God, why is this so hard?" Taking a deep breath, she closed her eyes and tried again. "I've only ever had sex once, and that wasn't anything like I'd thought it would be. In fact, it was downright disappointing. And the only time I've ever cli–climaxed was by myself."

"Look at me, baby," Cord demanded.

Shelby heaved another deep breath and opened her eyes. The heat of Cord's gaze caused her pussy to leak and clench.

"You don't have to worry about disappointment with us, Shelby. We are going to make you come so many times, you'll beg us to stop."

With hope flaring, she kept her gaze locked on Cord as he slowly lowered his head once more. Whimpering with pleasure as the tip of his tongue flicked over her sensitive clit, she bucked her hips up into his mouth.

"Oh yeah, you like having your pussy licked, don't ya, darlin'?" Brandt whispered against her ear, his warm, moist breath causing goose bumps to form on her hot skin. She didn't know if he expected an answer, but since she was beyond words she just moaned.

Cord slid his tongue down through the wet folds of her vagina, and then she cried out as he thrust his tongue into her wet hole. The slurping sounds he made as he sucked the cream from her cunt only turned her arousal up another notch.

"You taste so fucking good, baby. I want you to come in my mouth," Cord rumbled against her pussy.

"Oh God," she sobbed.

Brandt leaned over her and sucked on a nipple. Shelby felt like she had died and gone to heaven, and they hadn't even made her climax yet. She didn't know if she could stand much more of their attention without breaking apart.

Cord licked up the length of her slit and flicked his tongue back and forth over her sensitive bundle of nerves. When she didn't think she could stand any more of his ministrations without begging him to fuck her, he moved one of his hands and slowly pushed a finger into her pussy. Brandt released her nipple and covered her mouth with his, muffling her cry of pleasure.

Reaching up in desperation, she threaded her fingers into his black, silky hair and held him close. His tongue thrust into her mouth, and she twined hers with his. She sucked on his tongue, imagining what it would be like to have his hard cock in between her lips, the taste of his essence on her tongue.

Never before had she tasted anything as erotic as Brandt's and Cord's mouths. She didn't want to release Brandt's lips, but she couldn't draw enough air into her lungs through her nose, and the need for oxygen became paramount.

Her first deep breath came out as a scream of pleasure when Cord added another finger to her vagina and began to pump them in and out of her sheath, all the while laving her clitoris with his tongue. Familiar warmth traveled from her womb down her legs, up her stomach and torso, and into her arms. Curling her toes as the internal muscles of her pussy began to gather tighter and tighter, she gasped and mewled. Her uterus began to feel heavy, and molten lava traversed to her cunt.

"Ohgodohgodohgod. Cord, Cord, Cord," she chanted, only vaguely aware that she was speaking out loud.

All of a sudden she froze. Her body was so tight she was scared she would shatter. Her mouth opened on a silent scream as Cord rubbed a spot inside her she'd never felt before. Brandt bit lightly at one of her nipples and scraped the hard tip, and then she was flying. Shelby's whole body jerked and spasmed, her pussy clamped down on the fingers buried in her vagina, and she hurtled into space. Black spots formed in front of her eyes, and she cried out hoarsely, her pussy contracting and releasing as Cord kept thrusting his digits in and out of her, drawing out her orgasm until she didn't think she could take any more.

Muscles so lax with satiation that she didn't think she would ever move again, Shelby became aware of the growling and sucking noises Cord was making as he lapped up her cream. Her body still gave the occasional shudder and her pussy intermittently spasmed with sensitivity.

"Fucking delicious," Cord rasped breathlessly. Feeling him move, Shelby opened her eyes to look down at him. He pinned her with a gaze so heatedly intent, her just-sated vagina twitched with reawakening desire. The sexy bastard gave her a wicked grin, lifted his arm, and proceeded to suck clean the fingers he'd had buried in her pussy. She groaned and closed her eyes at such an erotically carnal act and didn't bother to open them when the mattress at her side dipped and bounced.

"My turn," Brandt growled. "I want me some of that pussy."

"Oh God." Shelby looked down at Brandt and realized he was naked. She didn't know he had stripped. He was so hot. He was hard and pumped but not overly so. The muscles in his arms, pecs, and stomach rippled as he moved. She couldn't see his cock, since he was already lying on his stomach between her thighs, but the man had an ass just begging to be bit.

Shelby moaned and drew in a ragged breath when Brandt moved between her legs and wrapped his arms around her thighs, pushing her legs up and out to bare her sex to his eyes.

"You are so fucking wet, darlin'. I can't wait to taste your cum. And when I'm done I am going to bury my cock in this sweet, pink little pussy. You will scream for me again, and after I've finished, Cord is going to fuck your cunt."

"I don't think…"

"That's right, baby," Cord interrupted. "Don't think, just feel."

Shelby whimpered at the first swipe of Brandt's tongue along her pussy. She was so sensitive that she didn't think she could handle what they planned to do with her. But Brandt surprised her. He didn't dive on her and devour her. The touch of his tongue was light, as if he knew just what she could and couldn't handle. Slowly, his light licks soothed her hot, delicate flesh and began to build her hunger. When she began to thrust her hips up at him, he applied more pressure, laving his tongue back and forth over her clit until she was sobbing with pleasure.

A gentle touch to her cheek made her turn her head and open her eyes. Cord was lying on his side, curled around the top of her head with his crotch close to her mouth. She had been so wrapped up in what Brandt was doing to her she hadn't realized where he was or that he had stripped out of his clothes.

He was so sexy. His skin was golden, and he had masculine chest hair between his pecs. Running her hand over his chest, her fingers curled in that soft, silky hair. The heat radiating from his body almost singed her skin. Smoothing her palm down his body, her eyes followed and caught on the huge cock bobbing with his heartbeat. It was long and wide with a dark, purplish-red head. Drool pooled in her mouth, the urge to taste almost paramount.

"I need to feel your mouth on my cock, baby." He grasped the base of his dick and ran the head over her lips. "Open up and suck me, Shelby," he commanded.

Shelby didn't have to be told twice. Reaching out, she wrapped her hand around the base of his hot, hard flesh, where his hand had just been, and leaned forward. She licked around the corona, groaning when she tasted his salty, sweet essence on her tongue. Opening her mouth, she covered the tip and sucked him in. His groan joined her hum, and she laved the underside of his dick with her tongue.

"Fuck, baby, your mouth is bliss," Cord gasped.

She hummed in reply and began to suck on him in earnest.

Shelby bobbed up and down the length of his cock, moaning and mewling out her own pleasure as Brandt continued to eat her pussy. He eased two fingers into her cunt, and she nearly shot off the bed when his fingers slid over her hot spot. She growled around the cock in her mouth.

"Yeah, Shelby, keep sucking my dick, baby," Cord groaned and gripped her hair. She wasn't sure if his hands in her hair were to keep her mouth on him or for him to anchor himself with. He didn't try to force his cock into her mouth and make her take what she couldn't. He just held her hair and stayed still, letting her take the lead.

Tears formed in her eyes at such a courteous and special moment. The one and only time she'd had sex, she had nearly been sick at the force used on her. Pushing those thoughts aside, she hollowed out her cheeks and slid back up his hard shaft, using her teeth to scrape over the sensitive head lightly.

"That is so fucking hot. I don't know how much more I can take," Brandt stated breathlessly.

"Me either," Cord replied, withdrawing his cock from her mouth as she sucked hard, trying to make him stay. "Send her over, Brandt. I want in that sweet, wet pussy."

Shelby squealed as Brandt dove back down to her cunt. He opened his mouth wide and sucked her clit in between his lips. Not once did he use his teeth on her and hurt her. Sliding his fingers in and out of her pussy, he massaged that spot inside her while nibbling, laving, and sucking on her clit with lips and tongue.

The buildup was fast and hard. She keened and gasped as her body raced to climax until she was there once more, on the edge of the precipice. Her breath hitched and froze in her throat, her mind shut down, and her body jerked as the orgasm hit powerfully. Body spasming and shuddering, she wailed as an intensive pleasure invaded her pussy, womb, and entire being.

Brandt didn't wait for her body to stop contracting. Instead, in the next moment she was gasping anew as he thrust his cock into her depths.

"Oh darlin', you are so fucking hot and tight. I just knew you were made for us."

Shelby whimpered as Brandt pushed his way through her tight muscles. He didn't forge through and hurt her, instead waiting until her still-contracting muscles released once more. Then he inched his way into her depths.

He covered her with his body but kept most of his weight on his elbows and began to rock in and out of her pussy. Shelby hadn't known such pleasure even existed. She'd heard when she overheard other girls talking, but to actually experience it was phenomenal.

Brandt started off slow, with just the slight advance and retreat once he was embedded all the way inside her body. She wrapped her legs around his waist and dug her heels into his fine ass as she caressed her hands down his back. Muscles rippled beneath her hands, sending her arousal even higher.

Every time he moved, the head of his cock dug at the spot inside her pussy, causing her internal muscles to clench.

"You like that, don't ya, darlin'," Brandt stated more than asked. "Imagine what it will feel like when you have both of us loving you at the same time. One cock in your pussy and another in your ass. We will make you scream so loud, darlin'."

Shelby gasped at his carnal, dirty words and groaned as he pushed up on extended arms and began to thrust his hips at her faster.

"You'd like that, wouldn't you, Shelby?"

"Oh God," she whimpered and then moaned when Brandt shifted again. His cock went so deep that she felt him against her womb. That little bump caused her to squeal with pleasure and close her eyes.

"Whatever you just did, she liked," Cord rasped.

"I bumped her cervix," Brandt said breathlessly.

Shelby's eyes flew open when Brandt moved again. He was sitting up between her splayed thighs, and he slid his hands under her ass and tilted her hips up. The new angle had his cock going much deeper, and as he pumped his hips forward again, he once more brushed her cervix. She couldn't contain her mewl of pleasure at the intentional touch.

"Fuck her harder, man, she likes her cervix to be bumped," Cord groaned.

"Oh. Ah," she grunted as Brandt did exactly that. "So good. Don't stop."

The tension in her body built higher and higher, causing her to buck and writhe. If it wasn't for the fact she was already close to climaxing again, Shelby would never have believed she could come again. She'd only ever been able to climax once a night by her own hands, so to speak, and to be on the verge of her third orgasm for the night blew her away.

"She's close, Cord. Her pussy is rippling around my dick, and I don't know if I can hold out. Help her over."

Cord caressed a hand down her belly and tapped her clit with a finger. She screamed and bucked in the throes of an orgasm so powerful she thought she would pass out. Her cunt clenched and released around Brandt's cock over and over again. Cream dripped from her pussy, and she saw stars. Then he surged into her twice more and froze. He roared when his cock expanded and flexed as he climaxed, spewing load after load of cum into her vagina.

Shelby came to with four hands soothing her arms, legs, and stomach. She must have passed out for a moment, because when she became aware of her surroundings again, Brandt was cleaning her up. She grunted and opened her eyes as the soft cloth connected with her sensitive folds.

"Are you okay, baby?" Cord asked.

"Yeah," she sighed. "Never better."

"Are you sore, darlin'?" Brandt queried.

"No. Just a little tender."

"Do you think you could take me, Shelby?" Cord inquired.

"Can I have a shower and then decide?"

"Sure you can, baby. You can have anything you want."

Cord moved off the bed, reached out, and scooped her up into his arms. Shelby sighed as she wrapped an arm around his neck and breathed in his clean, masculine scent. Her pussy clenched and released another drip of cream.

* * * *

Cord ground his teeth when Shelby sniffed his skin then licked his neck. He was in pain and couldn't wait to sink his cock into her pussy, but if she was too sore, he wasn't about to make her feel pressured to take him. Entering the bathroom which adjoined her room, he let her feet down onto the floor, reached into the shower, and turned on the taps. Checking the water to make sure it was at temperature, he then guided her into the large cubicle.

After washing her body, he rinsed the suds off and then quickly soaped himself up. While he had his eyes closed with his face beneath the stream of water, the little minx surprised him by wrapping her small hand around his cock and began stroking his hard length.

"Baby, you don't have to do that," he ground out.

"I know. I want to," she replied.

Cord clenched his fists to keep from reaching for her, lifting her into his arms, and impaling her on his hard, aching dick. Grasping her wrist, he withdrew her touch from his body before he embarrassed himself by shooting off.

He turned the water off. Helping her from the shower stall, he handed her a towel and kept his eyes off her delectable little body as he toweled himself dry.

"I want you to make love with me, Cord."

He froze. Every muscle in his body grew taut at her softly spoken words.

"Are you sure, baby? I don't want you to do that if you're too sore," he replied.

"I'm sure." She looked up into his eyes shyly and then down at his throbbing dick. "I can't wait to feel you inside me."

He glanced at Brandt as his brother smiled at him and stepped into the shower and groaned, then Cord lunged for her. He lifted her into his arms and practically ran back to the bed. With more patience than he felt, he sat on the edge of the mattress with her in his lap. Tilting her head up, he lowered his mouth and kissed her. She opened to him instantly when he ran the tip of his tongue over her lips and moaned when he thrust inside her mouth. God, she tasted so sweet, he couldn't get enough of her.

Weaning his mouth from hers, he once again connected their gazes and reached down between her legs. With slow, light deliberation, he ran the tip of his finger through her humid, slick folds. She closed her eyes and widened her thighs so he had easier access, and he didn't pass up the invitation. After making sure she was wet, he carefully thrust a finger into her cunt. She clenched on him, leaned back on his arm, and moaned.

Brandt came back from the bathroom and stood leaning against the doorjamb, watching.

Cord couldn't wait another minute. Shelby was wet and ready, so he had no compunction about turning her around on his lap until she was straddling his hips and thighs. Using the strength of his arms, he lifted her up until her pussy hovered above his hard cock.

"Tell me if it hurts, baby," he grated through clenched teeth and slowly lowered her onto his erection. "Oh fuck!"

Cord closed his eyes as her tight, wet flesh stretched and enveloped him. He grunted and tightened his hands on her hips, trying to keep still and give Shelby time to adjust to his penetration. His cock was only halfway in, and the urge to surge up into her until he was balls deep was nearly too much to control. Gasping in a breath, he eased his hold on her and lifted her back up until just the crown of his dick was inside her.

"More. I need more," she panted.

"Easy, baby. I don't want to hurt you."

"You won't. Now give it to me, Cord. Fuck me!"

"Oh God," he growled and thrust his hips up as he pulled her down.

When Shelby screeched, he froze. Releasing her hips, he caressed up and down her back. "I'm sorry, baby. So sorry. I didn't mean to hurt you."

"You didn't. You feel so good. Move!"

Cord didn't need to be told twice. Once more he gripped her hips. Using his arms, he lifted and lowered her onto his cock and he pumped in and out of her wet pussy.

"So fucking beautiful. So good," he gasped. "I'll never get enough of you, baby."

With every thrust of his hips and lift of his arms, he sped up the pace until the sounds of their flesh slapping together echoed around them. Cord grit his teeth and recited the twelve times tables, trying to control his body. He was so close to spilling inside her, but he didn't want to go over before she did.

"Brandt!" he called, knowing his brother wouldn't need another word to understand his command.

Brandt moved in behind Shelby and pinched her nipples. Her cunt shivered around his cock, making him clamp his jaw down harder. Then with practiced ease, his brother slid a hand down between his and Shelby's bodies, being careful not to touch him, and he massaged her clit and then stepped back. That was all it took. She threw her head back and screamed. The internal walls of her vagina clenched and then released, clamped and let go, massaging his erection and bathing him in her juices as she came. The tingling warmth at the base of his spine spread out and burned hotter, brighter than ever before.

His balls drew up and fire raced along his dick. He yelled as he shot her full of his cum.

Cord wrapped his arms around Shelby and held her close, soothing her down from her climactic high. She slumped against him and sighed, snuggling up close.

Cord was in love for the first and, he knew, the only time in his life. Never had anything felt so right and so rapturous. She was theirs, and she wasn't going anywhere.

Chapter Seven

The buzz of her alarm intruded into the best sleep Shelby had had since she couldn't remember. Without opening her eyes, she reached out, trying to locate the annoying noise to turn it off. Her hand connected with a warm, hard wall of muscle, and she opened her eyes, squinting to see where she was.

The remembrance of the previous night's episode of lovemaking caused her cheeks to heat with desire and uncertainty. She was embarrassed about last night's activities, but she didn't have enough experience to know how to handle the morning after.

"I'll get it, baby. Just stay there so you don't get cold." Cord's voice, gravelly with sleep, penetrated her foggy mind.

"It's my cell phone," Shelby stated. "I can't remember where it is."

Warm, muscular arms wrapped around her waist, and a nose nuzzled against her neck. "Hi, darlin', how did you sleep?" Brandt asked from behind her.

"Good. I can't remember the last time I slept so soundly." She snuggled back down, wiggling her ass into his crotch, and snickered when his hard cock nudged between her ass cheeks.

"Here you go, baby." Cord handed over her cell. The phone stopped ringing in the same moment that she wrapped her hand around it. She looked at the LCD display screen and surged up in the bed. The number was from her hometown of Bloomington.

"Shelby, what's wrong?" Brandt asked.

Just as she opened her mouth to reply, her cell began to ring again. Shelby scrambled over Cord and off the bed, stumbling as her legs threatened to give out. She made it to the bathroom, closing and locking the door behind her before she answered.

"Hello," she whispered.

"Ms. Richmond? Is that you?"

"Yes."

"It's Sheriff Percy Conan here, Shelby. I'm afraid I have some bad news."

"What?" was all Shelby could manage to get out as a lump of dread formed in her stomach.

"The authorities were transporting Ramone Perez to the maximum-security prison in Springfield. They wanted to make sure he couldn't escape the lower-security facility. His goons had been visiting too often, and the prison guards were worried he was planning an escape. It seems that Perez and his friends on the outside had indeed planned an escape. As of late yesterday afternoon, Ramone Perez is at large."

Shelby's knees buckled, and she slid to the floor next to the bathtub, only vaguely aware of the sheriff's voice droning on. *Oh God.* She was in deep shit. Ramone Perez had sighted her as he shot her brother, Ian. Shelby had wondered for months why he didn't just kill her, too.

The sheriff had suggested that Perez thought she was no threat. She was just one woman, after all, cowering behind the sofa. Hurrying to leave the crime scene, Perez had jumped back in his car with his cronies and driven off.

Except he had been caught. Later that night, he and the others were picked up by Bloomington PD in connection with an assault. Shelby learned, to her horror, that Perez had loaned money to Ian, money that Ian had lost gambling. When Ian couldn't pay, Perez had come for him and taken Shelby's parents, too.

The crime lab matched the bullet casings at the house with those in Perez's gun, but the key piece of the prosecution's case was Shelby's eyewitness testimony. Everyone connected to the case had praised her for helping to put a dangerous criminal behind bars for life. Shelby hadn't been too comforted by that. No one could bring back her family.

Once she'd done her part, she left town, running from her memories. Now Perez had escaped, and she had something real to run from.

"Shelby? Ms. Richmond, are you there?"

"Yes."

"Perez is seeking revenge. He talked about it to other inmates. It's possible that his man on the outside has been keeping track of you, too. Wherever you are, I think it would be best if you come back home, where we can protect you."

Shelby looked up when she heard a soft click as the lock to the bathroom door disengaged and then the doorknob turned. Cord entered the bathroom, took one look at her face, and reached for the phone.

"Who is this?" he asked and paused to listen. "Sheriff Conan, my name is Cord Alcott. I am an ex-cop and am part owner of a security company with my brother, Brandt, and cousins, Giles, Remy, and Brandon Alcott. We live in the small town of Slick Rock, Colorado, and as far as Shelby's safety and protection is concerned, I think she would be safer here with us. This town is a close-knit community with retired marines, cops, and special-force operatives as well as hard ranchers and local law enforcement.

"Can you fax or e-mail me everything you've got on this bastard?" Cord paused again. "Okay, thank you, Sheriff. Keep me updated, and I'll do the same."

Cord snapped the phone closed and squatted down next to her. Shelby was looking at him, but she couldn't understand what he was saying. Her ears were ringing, and she felt light-headed. Scenes from that horrible night flashed through her mind, and nothing seemed to make sense. Movement near the door drew her attention, and the buzzing in her ears intensified. Brandt was frowning at her and his mouth was moving, but she just shook her head. The light began to recede from her eyes, and she welcomed the darkness.

* * * *

"Shelby, what's wrong, darlin'?" Brandt asked when her saw her white, pinched face. He grew more concerned as he moved toward her. She was looking at him with a blank expression, and her pupils were pinpoints.

"Shit." Cord caught Shelby and pulled her against him before she slid sideways and her head hit the floor.

"What the fuck's going on?" Brandt yelled.

"We need to get her in bed, quick. She's in shock," Cord stated as he lifted her up into his arms.

"Fuck, she's so pale, Cord. I need her in my arms. I can't stand it when she's hurting so bad." Brandt pulled the covers back and got into bed.

Cord placed Shelby on the bed next to him, and he moved her onto her side and wrapped his body around hers. Her skin was cold and clammy, and Brandt didn't like it. He hated seeing her ill and scared.

Cord climbed in on the other side of Shelby, moving up close so that she was sandwiched between them, sharing their body heat.

"Tell me," Brandt demanded. He listened as Cord repeated everything he'd learned from the call from Sheriff Conan. Instantly, Brandt shifted into police mode. He filed information away, began making connections, tried to see the case as Sheriff Conan saw it. At the same time, fierce determination filled him. He looked at Shelby's pale face and resolved that nothing was going to happen to their woman.

"Okay, we can deal with this. There is no way in hell she's leaving our sight. We'll get Giles, Remy, and Brandon in to help protect her as well as Sheriffs Luke Sun-Walker and Damon Osborne.

And if that's not enough, we'll commandeer Damon's brothers Sam and Tyson, too."

"Don't forget about Britt and Daniel Delaney. They are two spooky dudes, but they're on our side. And I know Clay and Johnny Morten could take down a perp with a rifle without blinking an eye."

"I'll set up a meeting on Monday morning. We can distribute copies of Sheriff Conan's files." He looked back to Shelby's face, relieved that color was returning to her skin. "Right now we need to concentrate on Shelby."

"She's been through hell already, Brandt. We have to make sure she's seen the last of hell on earth."

Just then Shelby moaned and stirred. Brandt rubbed a hand up and down her arm, hoping his presence and touch were enough to keep her calm. He looked over at Cord and saw his brother brushing the hair back from her face and whispering in her ear. Even though he couldn't hear what his sibling was saying to Shelby, Brandt knew that he was reassuring her so she wouldn't wake up scared.

It seemed to work, because when she opened her eyes, the glazed, panicked look was gone and her body didn't tense.

"Are you okay, darlin'?"

Shelby turned her head to look at him, smiled, and gave a slight nod. Her eyes showed her unease, though. Brandt thought how strange it was that they knew all about the incident with Perez, first from overhearing Shelby tell Kayli and now from Sheriff Conan, but Shelby herself hadn't told them. He wished that she would. Not only would it be a token of her trust, but he thought that some of the anguish in her eyes would be released if she could just talk about it with them.

Now wasn't the time, though. No matter how long it took her to tell them, he and Cord would wait.

"We'll take care of you, baby. We won't let that bastard near you. I spoke with the sheriff from Bloomington, and he agreed that the safest place for you to be was right here with us. He is going to keep us in the loop, and he's put out an APB on Perez. That bulletin has been sent nationwide, so if Ramone pops up on the radar anywhere, he'll be back behind bars before he can blink."

"Thank you, Cord, Brandt. But the last thing I want is for you to be in the line of fire," Shelby stated emotionlessly. "I think it would be best if I went back home."

"Why?" Cord snapped.

Shelby disentangled herself from him and Cord then crawled off the bed. She pulled a robe on and then turned to look at them.

"Why do you think?" she asked without inflection and walked out.

Cord rose to his feet and jerked his jeans on. Brandt sighed and followed suit. It looked like their plans for the morning were flying out the window, but he didn't really care about that. What he did care about, or should he say *who* he cared about, was Shelby. And it seemed she was going to do her damndest to keep him and his brother out of the line of fire. God, she was amazing. Except there was no way in hell he was letting her leave and put herself in danger. The best way to keep her alive and safe was with him and Cord.

They found her standing motionless in the kitchen, looking out the window. "Shelby, be reasonable. You can't go back home. You don't know if Perez has friends watching your apartment and your parents' house. They could even be watching the sheriff's office, just waiting to follow you. Perez is after you. He's made that clear."

"You don't understand." She spun around to face him and leaned against the kitchen counter.

"Yes, we do, darlin'," Brandt said as he walked toward her. "What you don't understand is that we are trained to protect people and take down the perps. Have you forgotten what we did before the security company?"

"No. And I know you think you can keep me safe. But what if you can't? What if he comes after you to get to me?" she said with a hitch in her breathing. "I can't and won't live with that. Too many people have already died. Please, you have to let me go."

Brandt reached out and pulled Shelby into his arms as she broke down. For all that she was trying to keep her emotions at bay, their little woman cared about what happened to him and his brother. He looked over as Cord came up behind her and wrapped his arms around her waist. His face held just as much anguish as he imagined his did.

"Baby, you've got to stop worrying about everyone else except you," Cord said as he held her close. "You're the one in danger, Shelby. This town is full of very skilled law enforcement officers as well as retired marines and operatives. Please just calm down and listen to what we have to say. Then if you decide you want to go back to Bloomington, you can, but we will be coming with you."

"Come on and sit down, darlin'," Brandt said and guided her to the table. Once they were seated with fresh mugs of coffee, he and Cord began to explain that they were going to call on all the men living in Slick Rock. Then he told her about their intention of setting up a meeting first thing tomorrow morning. When they were done, they sat back and watched her as she processed the new information.

"It sounds like this place will have more than enough trained men to help out, but I don't want anyone else getting hurt because of me."

"Baby, you aren't the person causing trouble. You're not the one that went on a killing rampage. You have to get that sort of thinking out of your head right now. If you don't, you're going to make yourself ill. It's. Not. Your. Fault."

"Cord's right, Shelby. None of this is your burden," Brandt reiterated. "If you want to blame someone, then place the blame at the feet of Ramone Perez."

Shelby sighed and clutched the mug between her hands. Brandt didn't know if it was for warmth or to stop the trembling, but she clung to that mug like a lifeline. Finally she lifted her head and looked to Cord and then to him.

"Can I attend the meeting?"

"Are you going to stay?" Cord queried.

"Yes. You're right. I think my options will be better if I stay here." She took a deep breath. "But you better be prepared, because I have a feeling it won't be long before he finds me."

"Is that the only reason you're staying, darlin'?" Brandt asked, already knowing what the answer was. When Shelby lowered her eyes and shook her head, he felt the knot in his chest fade and his heart fill up with hope. He didn't push her to elaborate. Brandt didn't want her to feel pressured, but he knew then, in that moment, that Shelby was definitely the woman he and Cord had been waiting for.

Glancing up at his brother, he saw hope and love blazing out of his eyes before he concealed his expression. Brandt gave him a quick grin and then closed down his emotions when Shelby looked up at them. They had only just gotten her to agree to stay with them where they could protect her. Admitting their feelings too quickly would only send her running.

But that wasn't going to happen. Brandt was going to make sure she would never have to run from anyone ever again.

Chapter Eight

Shelby waited nervously for the men Cord and Brandt had told her were about to arrive. She'd outfitted the boardroom of the Slick Rock Security offices with a big urn full of coffee on a side table, along with cream, sugar, and some cakes and pastries she had bought from the diner. Glancing at her watch again, she noted that no more than a minute had passed since the last time she had looked.

Cord and Brandt had been in their office, on and off the phone, all morning. Now Brandt entered the room, giving her a smile and a wink, and began to place folders on the large table in front of the chairs. When he was done, he walked over to her, placed his hands on her waist, and pulled her in tight against his body.

"Why are you so jumpy, darlin'?"

Shelby craned her neck and quickly lowered it again as pain pulled along the tense muscles. "I don't know. It's just that I hate to be a bother. All of this is because of me."

"How many times do we have to tell you none of this is your fault, baby?" Cord asked as he entered the room, leaning into her back.

Shelby shivered with desire as their clean, masculine scents assailed her nostrils and their warmth wrapped her in comfort and desire. Her breath hitched and she gasped when Cord pushed his hips against the small of her back. The action drove her into Brandt, and she couldn't help but be aware of the bulge in his pants, pressing against her stomach.

Brandt groaned, nudged her chin up with a finger, moved back a little, and bent down. He covered her mouth in a hot, wet kiss, which set her body on fire. They hadn't made love to her since that first time, a couple of nights ago, and Shelby was craving their touch. She appreciated the fact they hadn't made a move on her again, since she had woken up sore, but now that she'd had their hands, mouths, and cocks in and on her, she needed to feel them again.

Whimpering with need, she tangled her tongue with Brandt's and lost herself in sensation. If it hadn't been for someone clearing his throat and interrupting, Shelby wondered how far Brandt would have gone. When he pulled back from her, he kept his arms around her waist and pulled her into his side. She looked up to see him grinning sheepishly at someone across the room.

"Shelby, this is Sheriff Damon Osborne and his brothers, Tyson and Sam," Cord said.

Shelby's head was spinning by the time the room was full of men. Some she had already met, and others she hadn't. There was Tom and Billy Eagle from the Double E Ranch and their good friend Sheriff Luke Sun-Walker, ranchers Clay and Johnny Morten, as well as Seamus and Connell O'Hara. Sitting next to the O'Haras were Britt and Daniel Delaney, and Giles, Remy, and Brandon were seated on the other side of the table. As she glanced about the room, her gaze touching on all the men, she noted how tall, muscular, and handsome they all were. None of the men in her hometown of Bloomington measured up to their masculinity, at least none of the men she had seen.

Turning back to the urn, she filled the rest of the mugs with coffee and placed them on the table. She had already moved the cream and sugar to the middle of the boardroom table.

"Come and sit down, darlin'," Brandt said and drew her with him, seating her between him and Cord. "Just let us talk things out, and if you have any questions, you can ask later. Okay?"

Shelby nodded and wondered what she was supposed to ask. She had no idea how this sort of stuff worked.

"I hear you have some business competition, Sam," Luke Sun-Walker said.

"Yeah, looks like, but to be honest I'm sort of glad that Quin and his brothers have set up business. I had so much work there was a backlog of more than three months," Sam replied.

"So you're not worried about the other mechanics setting up business in town?" Billy Eagle asked with a grin.

"Nah. The Badons are good friends of ours. They served alongside us. I know they won't hog business, and neither will I."

"They were marines, too?" Brandt queried.

"Yeah. We can call on them, too, if needed," said Sheriff Damon Osborne.

"That's good to know." Cord cleared his throat. "Okay, let's get down to business, gentlemen."

Cord and Brandt proceeded to outline the danger Shelby was in. They didn't sugarcoat the situation. In fact, by the time they had finished, she was even more scared than she had been to begin with. Cord pointed out that even though it was Ramone Perez who was the danger to her, he could also be using his gang members to help him get to her. And as far as he was concerned, that was a problem.

The information Sheriff Percy Conan had sent them only had some information on the thugs Perez ran with. God knows how many others the authorities didn't know about. Brandt went through the files, pointing out who would more than likely be working with Ramone, and even showed photographs of some of his cohorts, but what worried Shelby the most were the ones they didn't have information on.

"All right, that about wraps it up, gentlemen," Cord stated. "As soon as I get any updates from the Bloomington sheriff, I'll pass them over, but until then we have to keep vigilant. This asshole and his gang have a predilection for harming women. They don't care whether they are single or in a relationship, and they don't seem to have a fondness for a particular look. Tell your women so they are more alert, and I wouldn't let them go anywhere without one of you beside them.

"On the last sheet of paper in your folders you have a list of all our cell phone numbers. I suggest you program yours but most especially your women's cells with them. That way they can call on any of us for help if necessary.

"The new motel won't be leasing any rooms to anyone until this bastard is back in prison where he belongs, and neither will the club. As far as we are concerned, this town is on lockdown. If any strangers enter our home, we all want to know about it. Any questions?"

"Nos" were the answer as the men gathered their folders and began to file out of the room.

"Oh my God. What have I done?" Shelby groaned. If she'd had any idea what she was up against, she would never have agreed to stay. "I think I should leave. I can't be responsible for anyone else getting hurt."

"Shelby, none of this is your fault or your responsibility, sweetheart," Sheriff Damon Osborne stated as he rose to his feet. "You are not putting anyone else in danger. That asshole is. You won't be safer anywhere else. This town is full of military-trained men and hard ranchers, not to mention your men, who are ex-law, along with their cousins. We won't let anything happen to you or any of the other women in this town. Just make sure you do as you're told and are never alone. It'll all be over before you know it, honey."

Shelby watched as Damon left the room and slumped down in her chair. Cord reached out and lifted her onto his lap.

"Baby, stop torturing yourself. You're going to make yourself ill. I care about you, Shelby, and even if you hadn't decided to stay, I don't think I would have let you leave. I can't stand the thought of you not being here by my side."

"Really?"

"Cord's right, darlin'," Brandt stated. "So stop beating yourself up for something that is out of your control. You're where you're meant to be. With us."

"Now why don't we head on over to the diner for lunch. I can hear how hungry you are." Cord grinned when her stomach rumbled.

Shelby laughed and felt her cheeks heat slightly. "Okay. I could use something to eat. I was too worried and nervous to even look at the stuff I set out for breakfast."

"We noticed," Brandt replied, helping her up from Cord's lap. "Come on then, let's get some food."

* * * *

Cord watched as Shelby devoured her toasted sandwich and iced tea. He relaxed back in the booth and watched the tension she had been carrying around dissipate. He was glad that she was finally able to let her stress go. It had helped having Damon reiterate what he and Brandt had already told her.

Maybe now she would let them build on their relationship. Even though he and his brother had made love to her once already, Cord knew that Shelby had been holding part of herself back from them. Hopefully now she would let go and enjoy their time together more. As far as he was concerned, she was the only woman that would be by their sides for the rest of their lives.

Now all he and Brandt had to do was convince her that she was the love of their life and wouldn't be going anywhere. But that would have to wait until after she was safe once more, because he knew she wasn't going to commit to anything while her life was in danger.

He had worked her out so quickly. Shelby was hiding her true nature. She was an independent, sassy little thing but too scared to show her real personality. He'd seen glimpses of who she was, but now that the threat of the bastard and his thugs had spread, she was going to continue to hold herself inside. Their little woman was more worried about others than her own safety, and as far as he was concerned that had to change. She was the light of their lives. It didn't matter that she didn't really understand that fact right now. Eventually she would and come to accept that she was first in their relationship. If she wasn't happy, then how could he and Brandt be happy?

"Hey, Shelby," Felicity Morten called from across the aisle, where she was sitting with her husbands, Clay and Johnny. "When are you coming back out for another horse-riding lesson?"

"Um," Shelby started to reply and then looked to him and Brandt. Cord was glad she was looking to him and his brother for their opinion and direction. That was the only way they would be able to keep her safe.

"How about we come out Friday afternoon?" Cord suggested to the Mortens. "I think by the end of the week we'll all be glad for a bit of fun and relaxation."

"That sounds good to me," Felicity replied with a smile and looked to her men. "What do you two think?"

"That's fine, honey," Clay said. "Do you want to invite anyone else?"

"Ooh, I think that's a good idea. Why don't we make it a big get-together? That way Shelby can meet the other women. Leave it all to me, Shelby, and I'll give you a call."

When Clay leaned down and whispered in Felicity's ear, Cord knew he had said something dirty to his wife by the way her cheeks turned pink and she squirmed in her seat. He almost blew it right then and there by telling her how he felt when he saw the longing in Shelby's gaze as she watched the three people interacting but pulled himself back just in time. Now was not the time or the place. Holding in a chuckle as the Mortens called for their check, he watched as Johnny paid the bill and, with Clay's help, rushed Felicity out to their truck.

That's exactly what Cord wanted to do, but he and Brandt had too much work on their plate to play hooky for the rest of the day.

But tonight was a different story.

Chapter Nine

Brandt leaned back in his chair, replete from a great meal, and sipped his coffee. Shelby had cooked a great chicken casserole with fried rice as a side dish, and he had enjoyed every mouthful. Now all he wanted to do was take her to bed and love that sweet body. And if the look on Cord's face was an indication, his brother was feeling the same.

"Why don't you let Cord and I clean up, darlin'? Go and have a relaxing soak in the tub. When we're done we'll give you a massage and help you relax even more."

"Okay. Thank you," Shelby replied and left the kitchen.

Cord waited until she was out of earshot before he said, "She's still not talking, is she?"

"We can't let her keep hiding from us, Cord. You and I both know underneath that pleasant façade is a feisty vixen with a temper."

Cord nodded his agreement.

"I just wish she would trust us enough to let her out."

"I don't think it's us she distrusts. It's herself."

"Hmm, you may be right," Brandt speculated. "So what are we gonna do?"

"There's only one way I can think of," Cord stated as he loaded the last dish into the dishwasher and began to wipe down the counter.

"You mean…"

"That's exactly what I mean."

"Then what are we waiting for? We have a woman to love," Brandt said and headed out with Cord close on his heels.

Shelby was still in the bath. They could hear water splashing as she moved, and so Brandt and Cord began setting up for a night of lovemaking. While Cord placed towels on the bottom sheet to protect the material from any oils they used while they massaged her, he set up the fragrant candles around the room and lit them. The massage oil he had already placed on the bedside table along with a tube of personal lubricant. First they would make sure Shelby was relaxed, and then they would begin to caress and tease her sexy little body.

She would have to be prepared for what they had in mind, because Brandt wanted her to feel no unnecessary pain when they brought her to the brink of release over and over again. Hopefully she would get so frustrated she would become her feisty, normal self.

Once the room was ready Brandt went to the other bathroom and took a fast shower. Shelby still hadn't emerged by the time he came back.

Brandt was getting antsy and was just about to knock on the bathroom door when he heard the water draining from the tub. He concentrated on taking a few deep breaths to control his raging libido. This wouldn't go as planned if he made Shelby nervous with his intensity.

The door to the adjoining bathroom opened, and Shelby came out wrapped in a robe. She glanced about the room and smiled shyly. Stepping forward, Brandt took one of her hands and led her over to the bed.

"Are you ready for your massage, darlin'?"

"Yes. I've never had a massage before."

Brandt vowed then and there that it would become a ritual to give their little woman a massage at least once a week. Every woman should know the relaxed and supple feeling after having a rubdown.

"Take off your robe and get on the bed, baby," Cord directed from across the room.

Shelby kept her eyes lowered but did what he said. She stretched out on the towels on her stomach and waited.

Grabbing the oil, Brandt poured some into his cupped palm and handed the bottle off to Cord. He rubbed his hands together, heating the thin liquid so it wouldn't be cold on her bath-warmed skin.

After climbing onto the bottom of the bed, Brandt started working on Shelby's feet while Cord started on her shoulders. The little groans and moans she made caused his cock to throb and pulse against the fly of his jeans and heated the blood traveling through his body. He spent a considerable amount of time working on the tense muscles in her arch, and when they finally let go, he began to work his way up her calf. When he reached the top of her thigh, just inches away from her pussy, he switched to her other leg and worked his way back down. By the time he completed working on her other foot, Cord had reached the small of her back.

Shelby had stopped making noises about halfway through their manipulations, and her breathing had evened out to deep, relaxed breaths, but he knew she wasn't truly asleep. Their woman was so relaxed that she was dozing lightly. Glancing up to Cord, he gave his brother a nod. Now that they had her calm, it was time to begin loving her.

Brandt reached for the oil and coated his hands once more. This time, instead of working on one leg at a time, he smoothed his hands up the backs of both and continued on when he reached the fleshy globes of her ass.

She sighed and twitched when he kneaded her butt cheeks, but she didn't stop him. Brandt took that as permission to keep going. Using his large hands, he flexed her bottom open, stretching her anus without actually touching yet. Grinding his teeth to keep his moans of delight contained, he stared at her asshole every time he kneaded her open. That little brown-pink pucker was calling his name, and he didn't know how long he could go without fondling it.

When he glanced up and saw Cord eyeing her ass heatedly, he knew he couldn't hold out any longer. His brother was just as hungry for Shelby as he was. Leaning down as he held her open, he slowly licked from the top of her crack down. She whimpered but didn't draw away or protest. Finally he reached her ass and laved his tongue over the sensitive flesh. When the skin was moistened, he lifted his head and pushed against the tightly closed hole with the tip of a finger. Shelby moaned and didn't protest or flinch, so he massaged the skin of her ass until the muscles began to relax. With a patience he never knew he had, Brandt continued to caress until she opened up to him. Slowly easing the tip of his finger into her anus, he fought back the groan of desire bubbling up in his chest and throat.

"Do you like that, darlin'?" he rasped. "Do you like me playing with your pretty little asshole?"

"Yes!"

"Have you ever had anal sex, Shelby?" Cord rumbled.

"No!"

"Would you like to feel Brandt's cock fucking your ass, baby?"

"I–I d–don't know."

"We won't do it today, darlin', but eventually we are going to have our cocks buried in your gorgeous body at the same time," Brandt stated breathlessly. "I promise we won't hurt you. We are gonna make you feel so good, Shelby."

Brandt did groan this time. He finally had his finger buried in her ass as far as it would go. She was clenching on him so hard, he could just imagine how damn good her asshole would feel squeezing his cock.

"I can't wait," he panted and looked at Cord. His brother was looking just as feral with sexual need as he felt. Being careful not to hurt her, he withdrew his finger and cleaned it on the disinfectant wipe Cord handed him. Grasping Shelby's hips, he pulled until she had her ass in the air, giving him an unimpeded view of her wet pussy.

Shifting closer to her, he aligned his cock and rocked his hips forward. It took all of his control to not power into her with one surge.

Instead he waited for her body to adjust to the intrusion of his corona parting her slick flesh.

Shelby moaned with pleasure, her pussy clenching on him then releasing once more. Brandt was about to push a little more of his aching shaft into her vagina but didn't get the chance. She surged back against him and, squealing, took all of him with one reckless move of her hips.

Gripping her hips firmly, he gasped for breath. "Fuck, Shelby. I didn't want to do that in case I hurt you. Are you all right, darlin'?"

"More. I need more. Please?"

"We'll give you what you need, eventually, baby. Just let us love on you," Cord said in a steely voice.

"Shit!" Brandt cursed. He had been so caught up in Shelby, he had forgotten they were trying to get her to let go with them.

"Exactly," Cord growled.

"Okay, okay," Brandt sighed and ground his teeth. With single-minded devotion he began to rock his hips, sliding his cock in and out of Shelby's pussy. After five strokes he could already feel her internal walls rippling and knew she was close to orgasm. The poor girl wouldn't last another three strokes. Even though he hated doing it, he slowly eased his cock out of her warm, wet cunt and bit his tongue when she mewled in protest.

"What are you doing?"

"Making you feel good, baby," Cord ground out. "Turn over."

Shelby eyed first Cord and then looked over her shoulder at him. He didn't look away, and he let her see the desire he felt for her and a little of the love filling his heart. She gasped then frowned but did as Cord demanded.

When she was lying on her back, she looked from him to his brother expectantly.

"Move out of the way," Cord commanded, and Brandt did as he was told. His brother looked like he was on the brink of losing total control, but he knew better. When Cord was like this, it meant he was determined and would reach his goal, no matter who stood in the way.

Cord sat on his heels between her thighs, wrapped his arms around her legs, and spread her wide. He shifted back, lowered his head, and gave her one long lick with his tongue. His brother growled and gave her another lick from her pussy hole up through her soft folds and flicked his tongue over her clit. Shelby moaned and bucked her hips up, trying to get him to lave her little nub again. Cord lifted his head away from her vagina and kissed his way up her belly, taking the time to rim her navel, and then up to the underside of her breasts.

Shelby panted and moaned, bucking her body up and still trying to control where they touched her. Brandt didn't have to wonder for long how Cord would deal with that.

"Get the scarves from the closet."

Brandt did as his brother bid, and when he returned it was to see Cord suckling on one of Shelby's nipples while pinching the other. She looked so fucking sexy as she mewed with pleasure, her head tossing on the pillow.

"Restrain her hands," Cord commanded.

Brandt grabbed her wrists when she tried to slap his hands away, but he was a lot faster and more determined. Within moments he had the soft scarves around her wrists and then tethered her to the headboard, being careful not to hurt her in any way. She growled with frustration as she tested her restraints and found they held fast.

"Why?" Shelby snarled.

"You have to learn you aren't going to control us in the bedroom, baby. Plus you have to learn not to hold back with us."

"I'm not…"

"Don't lie to me, Shelby. Do you think we don't see how feisty you are? How passionate? You have a temper you are trying to hide from us, baby. Stop trying to control everything and let go, damn it!"

Shelby frowned, and then she looked concerned. When she closed her eyes and turned her head away, Brandt knew that Cord had gotten to her. But it irritated him that she still thought she could close herself off from them.

He climbed on to the bed and lay on his side, supporting his head on his hand. Watching her reactions, he ran a hand up and down her side and over her belly, slowly inching his way up to her breasts.

Cupping her fleshy globes in his hand, he swept his thumb over the hard peak of one breast and bent to take the other into his mouth. Inhaling, he sucked her hard nipple into his mouth and began to lave the peak with his tongue. Turning his head slightly so that he could watch Cord, he continued his ministrations and scraped his teeth lightly over her nipple.

Cord was once more comfortably ensconced between Shelby's thighs. He had her spread wide open, his hands keeping her legs from closing. From what Brandt could see and what he knew of his brother, Cord was licking all over Shelby's slit but not touching her clit. Even though she was trying to arch beneath them, he had removed his hand from her other fleshy mound and spread it over her ribs beneath her breasts. Cord moved his hand from one of her thighs, using his shoulders to keep her legs open, and placed his hand over her lower abdomen. There was no way she could escape them.

"Oh God. Touch me, please!"

Brandt released her nipple from his mouth with a pop. "We are touching you, darlin'."

"That's not what I mean, and you know it!" Shelby sobbed.

Cord lifted his head from her pussy. "Do you want to come, baby?"

"You know I do."

"Then stop holding back, Shelby."

"Fuck you."

Cord wasn't offended. He thought he glimpsed the spark of passion he and Brandt were looking for. "Oh, we will, baby, but not until you give all of yourself to us." Cord leaned down and began to lick her moist labia. He ran his tongue up and down her folds, over and over again, until she was gasping for air and her belly quivered. The sounds coming from her mouth let Brandt know they were getting to her. She sounded almost animalistic with her need.

This was what Cord and he wanted. They needed her to stop hiding behind her polite façade. Those two little words she had just spoken told him they were getting close.

Reaching over, he squeezed a nipple, watching her the whole time, not wanting to inflict any real pain, but he continued to press harder and harder. Her mouth opened and a growl emitted from between her lips and teeth, ending in an almost hissing sound.

"You like what we do to you, don't you, darlin'? Look at how your body tries to buck and bow, eager for more of our touch."

Brandt pinched a little harder. The keening sound she made had his cock jumping and his balls aching. He so wanted to pick her up and impale her on his hard dick, but until she gave them what they wanted, that wasn't about to happen.

Shelby sobbed with each exhalation as Cord began to give her clit a little flick with each lick of his tongue. Her body was so taut with sexual tension that he wondered if she was going to snap.

Releasing her hard nipple, he leaned over and laved the peak. She tugged against her restraints, but he knew she wasn't going to be able to move those hands from where they were tied. He ran a finger beneath the material, checking that she wasn't cutting off her circulation. The scarves were soft and stretchy enough not to do any damage to her silky skin.

"I can't take any more. Please?" she begged.

"What do you want, baby?" Cord rasped after lifting his mouth slightly away from her pussy.

"I want you to fuck me. I want you both to fuck me, and I want it *now*!" Shelby screamed.

"I am not going to fuck you, baby, but I will make love with you. We both will," Cord said between ragged breaths.

Brandt saw the moisture in her eyes before she closed them. They were definitely getting to her.

"Open your eyes, darlin'. Don't you dare hide from us."

When she didn't open them straight away, Cord slapped his hand down on her pussy. She screamed and writhed as if she was in agony, and Brandt was afraid his brother had gone too far.

Chapter Ten

"Again. Oh God, do that again," Shelby cried.

Her pussy was on fire. If anyone had ever told her she would be nearly orgasmic from a slap to her pussy, she would have told them they were crazy. The internal walls of her sheath were spasming consistently, and cream was leaking from her in copious amounts.

Since the moment they had her naked on the bed, they had been torturing her with pleasure. Shelby hadn't even realized she was holding back from them until they had told her. She had kept herself bound up so tightly over the last six months, afraid she would snap if she didn't, and now they wanted her to let go and be herself.

I will make love with you. Cord's words swirled in her thoughts. They made the ice casing around her heart begin to crack and melt. Did that mean they loved her? She was too afraid to ask, and there was no way she was telling them how she felt. Her heart couldn't stand another loss, especially not of these men.

"I don't want this. You have to stop."

"What are you thinking, Shelby?" Cord asked quietly, and it was only then she became aware of the tears running down her cheeks.

Brandt quickly untied her wrists and massaged her arms as he lowered them. He picked her up and scooted further onto the bed so he was leaning against the headboard with her on his lap.

Cord shifted closer and rubbed a hand up and down her leg.

"Talk to us, darlin'." Brandt rubbed her back. "Let go of whatever is hurting you. If you don't, it will continue to eat away at your insides."

She looked from Cord to Brandt and back again and then lowered her eyes as she gathered her courage.

"Look at me, baby," demanded Cord, reaching out and gripping her chin between thumb and finger.

As she looked up again, she couldn't contain her gasp of surprise when she saw so much emotion looking back at her.

"That's right, Shelby. I love you, baby. I will do anything to make you happy, and if that means holding back from giving you orgasms and making love with you, then I will. You have to stop torturing yourself with the past. There was nothing you could have done to save your family. I thank God every day that the cops came at the right time, otherwise you could be dead as well. You mean everything to me. I won't put up with you only giving us pieces of yourself."

"I didn't...I wasn't..."

When she didn't go on, Brandt said, "I love you, too, darlin'. Please give us a chance? We want all of you, Shelby, not just what you think we like. We know you have faults. God, neither of us are perfect. Cord is a control freak, and I am always the one trying to be the peace maker. No one is infallible, darlin'. Please talk to us."

The love they felt for her shone from their eyes. Shelby's tears began to fall faster and faster, and then she couldn't contain them at all. Turning her head into Brandt's chest, she sobbed for the horrific loss of her family. Finally, when the tears stopped, she reached for the handkerchief Cord handed her, wiped her face, and blew her nose.

Then she began to talk. Though she knew they had heard her tell Kayli, though she knew they'd learned even more in their effort to protect her from Perez, she had to tell them herself. It all came out, from seeing Perez's face in the window to the way she'd run to the nightmares that continued to plague her. Her men let her talk without interruption, but she had their total attention. They kept their hands on her, reassuring her with their touch. Their love and support was almost palpable. Though Shelby still feared what might happen to them if Perez tracked her down, she realized just how grateful she was to have them here.

By the time she had finished, she was lying down on the bed in Brandt's arms with her head resting on his chest. Cord had moved into her back, cuddling her from behind, and the covers had been pulled up. Shelby couldn't seem to stop yawning. Even though she was still horny and wanted her men to make love to her, she just didn't seem to have the energy anymore. Her eyelids were getting too heavy to keep open.

"Close your eyes and sleep, darlin'. You need to rest. We will talk more tomorrow." Brandt kissed her head, pulling her in tighter against his body. Her mind, body, and heart felt a lot lighter now that she had talked out her problems. She wanted to reciprocate and tell them she loved them, too, but still she hesitated.

Her convoluted way of thinking was telling her to hold off. If she told them she loved them, then that would make this relationship real. And she didn't want to have to face any guilt if Perez tracked her down and one of them got hurt because of her. Maybe tomorrow she would have the courage to tell them.

Cord wrapped an arm around her waist and pulled her ass into his groin. He kissed her shoulder and sighed. That was the last thing she knew until morning.

* * * *

After showering and dressing, Shelby made her way to the kitchen, where she could hear the low rumble of Cord's and Brandt's voices. She hesitated in the kitchen doorway, not sure how they would treat her after what she had revealed the previous night.

"Hey, baby, how did you sleep?" Cord walked toward her, took her hand in his, and led her to the table. He handed her a mug of coffee after she was seated.

"I slept really well."

"You sound surprised, darlin'. Did you think you would have more nightmares?" Brandt asked as he placed a plate of scrambled eggs and toast on the table in front of her.

Shelby looked up at him with a frown.

"Why do you care if I have nightmares?"

"Because we care about you, baby. Don't you get it yet that we love you? We told you that last night."

She looked at Cord then Brandt and looked down. "I'm sorry. I didn't want to disturb either of you."

"You didn't, darlin'." Brandt brought two more plates to the table. "We have been trained to be aware of our surroundings. Habits are hard to break. Eat your breakfast."

They ate in companionable silence. Her heart was full of hope since they hadn't turned away from her now that they knew what she had been hiding inside. Those three words were on the tip of her tongue, but she held them back. She needed more time to be sure of what she felt, plus there was still a threat to her and, in her mind, to her men as well. She wouldn't feel comfortable until they were all safe. When she'd had her fill, she pushed her half-empty plate away and sipped her coffee.

"You don't eat enough, baby. How do you expect to last through the day without having a good breakfast?" Cord pointed toward her plate.

"I've eaten more here than I ever have before. I never ate breakfast before I came here."

"Well, at least you're eating something, I guess. We have to head out soon, are you nearly ready?" Brandt began to clear the table.

"Let me do that. You guys cooked breakfast." But Brandt wouldn't let her clean up by herself, so they worked together, and before long the kitchen was tidy. "I just need to brush my teeth and get my purse, then we can go."

When they were on their way to work, Shelby realized she hadn't been contacted by the Badon brothers regarding her car. She decided that she would call them as soon as they got to the office. They should have contacted her before now.

Cord and Brandt were in their office, so as Shelby waited for her computer to boot up, she picked up the phone and dialed.

"Badon Mechanics, Quin speaking."

"Oh hi, Quin. It's Shelby Richmond. I was wondering what was happening with my car?"

Quin was silent for several moments, and then he cleared his throat as though he was uncomfortable. "Haven't Cord and Brandt talked to you?"

"No. Should they have?"

"Um, well, okay. The thing is, Shelby, that your car is a mess. You have a cracked manifold, a blown head gasket, the rings need to be bored, the radiator is shot, and the thermostat is stuck open. The sump is leaking oil, the suspension is shot, and your back window is unroadworthy."

"Uh…" Shelby hesitated, not sure she understood everything. "Can you fix it?"

"Well, I could, but you'd be up for thousands of dollars, sugar. Your best bet would be to get a new car."

"But I can't afford a new car. Shit, what am I supposed to do now?" She sighed. "Wait a minute. Are you telling me that Brandt and Cord knew about my car?"

"Um, er, maybe you should go and talk to them, sugar."

"Oh, believe me, I will. Thanks, Quin." She wondered how long they had known about her car problem. *Why would they hide that from me?* Shelby was so angry she was shaking with it.

"No problem, Shelby. Just let me know if you need anything else." Quin hung up.

Shelby stared at the receiver in her hand. What would she need Quin for? From the sound of things, there was nothing he could do to help her out.

After replacing the receiver, she spun her chair around and looked into the office. Brandt and Cord were both on the phone, so she couldn't very well barge in there and give them a piece of her mind right then. She was going to have to wait, and Shelby knew that was not a good thing. The more she waited to vent, the angrier she became. How the hell was she going to confront them about her car without blowing things all out of proportion? They probably had a valid reason for not letting her know about her car problems. But right at this moment she couldn't figure out what it might be. She felt a twinge of panic when she imagined Perez coming after her. There would be no way to run, no way to draw him away from Cord and Brandt. She wasn't sure which made her angrier, that she'd gotten so complacent as to let this happen or that the men had trapped her here.

Brandt hung up the phone and looked up at her. He gave her a smile and a wink, and she narrowed her eyes at him. Sliding her gaze over to Cord, she caught him watching her with a frown.

Leaning back in her chair, she crossed her legs, folded her arms beneath her breasts, and shot daggers at them. Brandt's smile turned to a frown. Cord's eyes narrowed to slits, and she saw him clench his jaw.

Finally Cord hung up the phone and kept her pinned with his eyes. Shelby wanted answers, and she wanted them now! Rising from her chair, her arms still crossed, she stormed across the carpet and entered their office.

"Who the hell do you think you are? Who gave you the right to make my decisions and try and run my life?" she spat, pointing a finger at both men.

"What the hell are you talking about?" Cord snapped just as his cell phone rang. He held up a finger, indicating for her to wait. Shelby clutched her folded arms with her hands and began tapping her foot as Cord spoke into the phone.

"Yeah...hmm, okay that explains it...you could say that. Thanks, man, I owe you." Cord disconnected the call and stared back at her. "Explain."

That was all it took for Shelby to lose control. She ranted and raved, glared and pointed her finger at one man and then the other. By the time she had finished she was breathing heavily and couldn't remember what her runaway mouth had just spouted. *Oh shit, did I just call them ignorant swine and controlling assholes?* Not that there was anything too bad in that, but from the way they were both looking at her they weren't too happy, but they weren't angry either. *What's up with that?* Shelby tried to recall what else she had said, but when she was on a rant, which she hadn't let out for so long, she never remembered everything her runaway mouth spurted. "Motherfucker" kept ringing through her head. No, surely she hadn't.

"Sit. Down. Now," Brandt commanded softly.

Shelby flinched but decided discretion was the better part of valor, even though she was still angry, and sat in one of the chairs across from their desks. She had never heard that tone from Brandt before, and even though he was probably angry and had every right to be, his heated control turned her on. Clasping her legs tighter, trying to circumvent her aching clit, didn't help one little bit.

She studied Brandt's face, and even though he didn't look angry, his face was an expressionless mask. Then she looked into his eyes and saw the gleam in them. He might not be happy about her verbal tirade, but he was happy she had lost control. Shifting her eyes to Cord, she saw the same glint in his eye, and she thought she saw his mouth twitch. She looked back to Brandt when he took a deep breath.

"A. You will not flinch away from us. We would never hurt you, but that doesn't mean we won't get angry," Brandt said quietly. "B. It's about fucking time you let the real Shelby out. We are glad to finally see her, and don't you dare try and hide from us again, but you still don't have the right to speak to us that way."

"C." Cord took over. "The reason we didn't tell you about your car was because we didn't want you worrying about how to come up with the money to pay for repairs when it should be on a scrap heap. You had enough on your mind without another incidental problem. D—don't you dare interrupt, we haven't finished." Cord rose from his chair and moved around to the front of his desk to lean back against it with his arms still crossed.

Brandt drew her gaze as he, too, moved out and leaned next to Cord. Obviously they were trying to portray a united front.

"I know to you not having a car is a major concern, but since we all work and live together it didn't seem like too much of a problem. You have a lift to and from work every day. If you had wanted to go somewhere by yourself, all you had to do was ask and we would have handed over the keys or taken you ourselves. We already told you if you wanted to go back to Bloomington that we wouldn't stop you. In fact, if I remember it right, we told you we would come with you. But you decided to stay, and since you seemed content to let us drive you around and we like doing it, we didn't think anything of it.

"When Quin called and told us how bad your car was, we knew it was going to cost way too much money to fix, so we told him to leave it be. We had plans to surprise you with a new car when you accepted having a relationship with us. But if you decide you'd rather waste money on a heap of junk and spend God knows how long trying to pay it off, you go right ahead, baby."

Shelby felt the tension begin to leave her body. Taking a deep breath, she processed what they had just said. She still wasn't happy about not being told about her car, but she had also been lax in that regard. In fact, she had become so comfortable around them, having them drive her to and from work, she had completely forgotten about her junk heap. And now that she was back in control after venting her anger, she realized she had ruined what was supposed to be a surprise after she had insulted them both.

"I'm sorry. I shouldn't have lost my temper."

"Don't you dare apologize for being human, Shelby. We all lose our temper sometimes, and I, for one, am glad you are finally letting the real you out." Brandt smiled at her.

"I still shouldn't have vented the way I did. When I get angry like that my mouth runs away and I can't remember half of what I've said. I'm sorry I ruined your surprise." She looked at Cord.

She was surprised they were considering spending that much money on her when she hadn't even told them she was prepared to stay in Slick Rock yet. The thought of them looking after her and buying her a new car so she wouldn't be driving a death trap touched her deeply.

"Baby, you don't need to worry. We could go out and buy ten cars without even batting an eye." Cord stood up and walked over to her. He held a hand out toward her, and she placed hers in his. Pulling her to her feet, he brought her up against his body and hugged her.

"Well, I don't care if you can. I don't want you spending your money on me when it isn't necessary."

"You are a sweetheart." Brandt came up behind her and hugged her, too.

Shelby felt like she was home. Now, if only she knew how to tell them that.

Chapter Eleven

Shelby peeked through the window into Cord and Brandt's office. Cord was on the phone and Brandt was concentrating on his computer, but she caught their eye and gave them a wave, pointing toward the front door to indicate she was going to the diner to pick up their order for lunch. Cord waved back and Brandt smiled. Shelby still felt slightly chagrinned after her outburst this morning, but now she felt like they were on a more solid footing than ever before.

Giving them a wave, she made her way outside. The small town was busy with activity, and she inhaled the clean, fresh air. Looking up the road both ways to make sure it was clear, she stepped off the curb and began to cross. Hearing a squeal of tires and a throb of bass, she looked up to see a car bearing straight for her. She leaped across the road. She turned her head to look at the idiot driver in the souped-up car with a subwoofer polluting the air as he sped past. The man looked familiar, but she couldn't remember where she had seen him before. She reached the opposite curb, but her foot landed awkwardly and her ankle gave way. As she fell to the ground, she cried out, startled. Men came rushing toward her from everywhere, asking if she was all right and where she was hurt.

Shelby felt crowded and wanted them to back off but bit her tongue since they were only trying to help her. Then all of a sudden they were gone. The shadow of a large man fell over her as the sun silhouetted his frame from behind. Then he squatted down, and she exhaled with relief to see Sheriff Luke Sun-Walker.

"Are you all right, Shelby? Are you injured?"

"No. I'm fine. Just a little shaken," she sighed. "Some people shouldn't be allowed to have a license."

Luke's mouth quirked as he held back a smile. He offered his hand to help her up. "Amen to that."

With her ankle throbbing, Shelby tried to contain a wince of pain as Luke helped her to stand, but he must have seen it. He bent down and picked her up in his arms. "Where are your men?"

"At the office. I'm fine, you know. I can walk."

"That may be so, but I don't want you doing more damage than necessary." He carted her through the door to the diner and seated her at the edge of a booth. He pulled his cell off of his belt and hit speed dial.

"Luke here. Shelby's had a slight accident, but she's okay. Yeah, we're in the diner. Right, see you in a sec." Luke ended the call. "They're on their way."

Shelby turned her head to look over her shoulder, and sure enough, Brandt and Cord came barreling out of the building across the street and ran toward the diner. They looked absolutely frantic. She wanted to go to them and reassure them, but her ankle was throbbing like a bitch and she wasn't sure if she could put any weight on it.

The door to the diner slammed open just as Luke bent down to examine her ankle. She flinched but wasn't sure if it was a reaction to the loud noise or because Luke was probing her already-swelling skin.

"Shelby, my God, are you all right? What happened, baby?" Cord blurted with concern as he and Brandt knelt at her feet, effectively shoving Luke out of the way.

"We need some ice," Brandt yelled toward the counter.

Shelby told them what happened and then looked toward Luke. "Did you see that idiot?"

"No. The car was already out of sight before I got to you. You need to get her to the doctor's office. That ankle's too swollen already and starting to bruise She probably has a fracture or a bad sprain."

A few people in the diner piped up and told them what they'd seen from inside the building. One man said it had looked like the bastard had been aiming for her. She shivered with apprehension then pushed that aside.

"I thought he looked familiar," Shelby said quietly, "but I don't know why I think that."

"It could have been one of Perez's cronies," Luke suggested.

"Did you see all the photos at the meeting that we called, Shelby?" asked Cord.

"I'm not sure. I'll have to take another look."

"We can deal with that after you've been to the doctor's, baby," Cord stated.

Brandt took a clean towel wrapped around ice from one of the waitresses and placed it around her ankle. Shelby hissed.

"Sorry, darlin', but this will help with the pain and swelling. Cord, go and get the truck. We need to get her ankle seen to."

"On it."

"I'm right here, you know," Shelby said belligerently. "I'm not deaf."

"I know that, darlin', but we're worried about you."

She rolled her eyes and looked about. Her cheeks heated when she saw that nearly every eye in the place was on her. A few of the men gave her smiles and winks. The women looked concerned but smiled when they caught her looking back. Shifting in her seat, she tried peering around Brandt, but he grasped her chin and brought her gaze back to him.

"Are you sure you're okay, darlin'? You're as white as a sheet."

"Fine," she answered through gritted teeth. The pain in her ankle was awful, and she was having a hard time dealing with it. Just as she was about to push Brandt's hands and the ice pack away from her skin, the door to the diner once again burst open.

"Come on, let's get you to the doctor's," Cord said and gently picked her up. He carried her out to his truck, which was double-parked, the hazard lights blinking.

"Get in the back." Cord nodded at Brandt. "I want you to guide her foot in so she doesn't get hurt."

Brandt and Cord got her settled with her leg resting across Brandt's thighs. Moments later Cord was driving to the doctor's.

The doctor met them at the door and told them the sheriff had called ahead. Cord carried Shelby into the exam room and placed her on the bed.

"Okay, little lady, I need to get your shoe off. I'll try not to hurt you too much," the doctor told her as he undid the laces to her shoe.

Shelby clenched her teeth and couldn't prevent a whimper of pain escaping as he removed her shoe and sock. She felt a bit silly with the leg of her slacks folded up to her knee but was in too much pain to care overly much.

"Well, now, I think an X-ray is definitely in order." The doctor looked to Cord. "Can you carry her out and into the other room?"

Cord picked her up again, and Shelby draped her arm around his neck. He maneuvered the way carefully through the door and into the room opposite.

"All righty, now. Put her on the bed over there while I set up the machine."

Cord placed her on the bed while the doctor rearranged the machine. When he was done he ordered the Alcott brothers from the room and stepped behind the radiation screen. He was about to push the button but popped his head out to look at her.

"Is there any chance you're pregnant?"

Shelby thought back to the night she'd had sex with her men for the first time and realized they hadn't used any protection. Since she wasn't on the pill, there was a possibility she had conceived. She bit her lip and nodded her head. The doctor picked up a large gray-looking apron and placed the heavy object over her. It covered her from chest to knee.

Moments later the doctor had taken the X-ray and walked over to her. "It will be a few minutes before the film is ready. Do you want me to do a pregnancy test?"

"Yes, but I don't want them to know about it."

"Okay, you just leave it to me," he replied.

The doctor called Cord back to carry Shelby into his office then ushered him and Brandt out again when he said he was going to give her a Pap smear. They lit out of the room so quick, she nearly burst into laughter.

"Well, there now. That was easy," the doctor said with a smile, and this time Shelby giggled.

The doctor helped her into the bathroom and left her with a pregnancy test kit. Shelby had trouble moving since she could only place weight on one leg, but she got the job done. After washing her hands she opened the door, handed the stick to the doctor, and after he had placed it into a metal dish, he helped her to a chair.

"All right. You are definitely pregnant. Congratulations," he said after glancing at the stick. "You'll need to get this prescription for prenatal vitamins filled. I want you to come back in a month's time for a checkup. Do you need help to tell the father?"

"No," Shelby whispered in shock. She felt the blood drain from her face and cursed her stupidity. *Why the hell didn't you ask them to use a condom? Because you were too caught up in the moment to even think of protection. You are such a dumb-ass, Shelby! How could you be so stupid?*

"Are you all right with this, Shelby?"

"Um. I wasn't planning on having a baby, and it was a bit of a shock. But I love the thought of holding my child in my arms," she replied with a small smile. Shelby realized then that she was more than okay with being pregnant. The thought that she had conceived Cord and Brandt's baby filled her up with hope and joy. She hoped like hell they would be just as pleased before realizing that she might have a bigger problem than that. Perez was out there, searching for her. Her happiness faded. She wasn't even sure if she could protect herself, much less an unborn baby. If she told the men, they'd feel even more responsible for her safety and even more likely to put their own lives on the line for her.

The doctor went to get the X-ray films, put them up on the bright screen, and studied them carefully. After much scrutinizing, he turned the screen off and sat back across from her.

"Well, you'll be pleased to know you haven't broken or fractured your ankle. But you do have a bad sprain. You're going to have to keep off the ankle for at least a week, so I'll go and get you some crutches in a moment." He paused. "Since you're pregnant, the only pain medication you can have is Tylenol, and sparingly. I'm afraid you're just going to have to bear most of the pain. Place ice packs on that ankle every twenty minutes for ten minutes at a time, and keep it elevated. That will help with the pain. Any questions?"

"No. Thanks, Doctor."

"Don't thank me, I'm just doing my job. Call me if you have any concerns. I'll send your men in while I get you some crutches."

The doctor opened the door and admitted Cord and Brandt. She explained that she had a sprain and needed to keep off that leg.

"Thank God, it's not broken," Cord said with relief and looked up as the doctor came in with the crutches.

"Now, remember to rest up, little lady, and no weight on that foot."

Shelby tested the crutches. Since she had never used the apparatus before, she felt rather uncoordinated, but she knew she would eventually get the hang of them. She made her way toward the parking lot, albeit slowly, with Brandt walking on one side while Cord took up the rear. She was thankful, because she wobbled a couple of times and they steadied her with their hands.

"Okay, let's get you home," Cord said after she was in the back of the truck, once more with her leg resting across Brandt's lap.

"No, we can't go home. I need to get back to the office. I still have work to do."

Cord turned around to face her from his place in the driver's seat. "Don't you dare argue about this, Shelby! The doctor said you were to rest up and keep your weight off of that foot. You can't sit in an office comfortably. There is nowhere for you to prop your foot up or lie down if you need to."

Shelby bit her lip and looked away as Cord turned back, started the truck, and headed home. She knew he was right, but she felt a bit guilty. Not only was she hiding her pregnancy from them, but she couldn't work now. She hadn't been working for them long enough to accrue any sick leave. Well, she would just have to take time off without pay. She didn't have much choice, and the pain in her ankle was making her feel sick to her stomach.

Cord carried her into the living room and placed her on the sofa. He propped a cushion beneath her calf while Brandt went to get an ice pack and painkillers from the kitchen. While she took the pills, Cord wrapped her ankle with the ice pack.

"I'm really sorry, baby, but I have to get back to the office. There are a few things I still need to do before I can call it a day. Brandt will stay with you and keep you company. I'll bring those photos home for you to look over later. Why don't you try and have a nap?"

"I'll be fine by myself," she said. "You don't need to hover. I have crutches here if I need to anything."

"No fucking way, Shelby. We aren't leaving you alone. You haven't learned how to use those things properly yet. You could fall and hurt yourself more." Cord leaned down and kissed her cheek. "I love you, baby. I need to know you're being looked after."

Shelby closed her eyes and savored his touch. She wanted to tell him how much she loved him, and Brandt, too. But she wasn't sure how they were going to react once she told them they were going to be fathers, and that uncertainty made her hold back the words.

"Get some rest, Shelby. I'll get takeout on the way home." Cord brushed a finger down her cheek and left.

"Do you want to watch a movie, darlin'?" Brandt asked as he turned on the entertainment system.

"Sure."

Brandt put a movie on and then sat beside her on the sofa. He moved into the corner so she wouldn't disturb her leg and pulled her body in close to his. Her back was now resting against his chest and side, with her leg stretched out along the couch, propped up on the cushion. She settled deeper into his embrace, his arm wrapped beneath her breasts, and turned to watch the action on the screen.

* * * *

Brandt watched Shelby's struggle to keep her eyes open. The movie had just started, and he knew she wouldn't be able to stay awake to see much of it. As her eyelids slid closed, he turned the sound down low and gently shifted her head into a more comfortable position against his chest. When her breathing deepened and evened out, he knew she had finally fallen asleep.

He had been so scared when Luke's call had come in and told him Shelby had had an accident. His heart had nearly burst out of his chest as it raced with fear. Even now that he had her safe in his arms, he wanted to hunt down the stupid dumbass who had caused her to get hurt.

Brandt didn't care what was on the television screen. He was content watching Shelby as she slept in his arms. Holding her reassured him that she was alive and well. He felt sorry for Cord. His brother was a control freak, and if he had his way, Shelby would now be tied to their bed for the entire duration she was injured.

The thought of Shelby going toe-to-toe with Cord and himself turned him on. And after she had finally let go with them this morning, letting them have it with both barrels, he couldn't wait for her to lose her temper again. It seemed that once Shelby let loose, she let loose in a big way.

Their little woman had looked so wild. Her cheeks had flushed a pretty pink, fire had blazed from her eyes, and her hair had swung around her head as she gesticulated wildly with her hands and arms. God, she was magnificent. As he had watched her, his dick had engorged so fast, it was a wonder he hadn't passed out from lack of blood to the head.

She had finally let her true, passionate nature out, and as far as he was concerned she wasn't going to go back into hiding. Occasionally, he and Cord would like to dabble in a little play before they made love to her.

There was no way they would do that now. Not with her injured. He looked down at her sleeping face and stroked her hair back from her forehead, filled with the desire to protect her. As far as he was concerned, there would be no lovemaking until she was fully healed.

His cell phone vibrated. Carefully extracting it from the clip on his belt, he looked at the text from Luke.

The car which nearly hit Shelby was found abandoned outside of town. It was reported stolen two days ago. Will dust for prints but don't hold out much hope of finding any leads.

"Shit," Brandt muttered and sent a reply. *I don't like this. Did you tell Cord?*

Yeah.

Keep us informed.

Brandt had a bad feeling in his gut and didn't like it one little bit. He was worried that Perez or one of his goonies had found where Shelby was.

Chapter Twelve

"It was Perez," Shelby gasped and struggled to her feet. She was carefully working her way toward the kitchen, where Brandt was making coffee, on her crutches.

"Did you say something, darlin'?"

"Yes." She leaned against the doorjamb as he turned toward her. "The man in the car was Perez. He's changed the color of his hair and has shaved off his beard and mustache. That's why I didn't recognize him straight away."

Brandt moved toward her and removed the crutches from her hands, but he kept his hand at her elbow to keep her steady. After leaning them against the wall, he picked her up and carried her back to the living room and sat down with her on his lap.

"We'll keep you safe, darlin'," Brandt said as he hugged her tight. "He'll have to get through us to get to you."

That's what I'm worried about most. God, how do I keep them and our baby safe? If she had the means and wasn't injured, she would have packed up and left right away. Even though she knew she would hurt them, it was better than them being injured or, even worse, dead.

* * * *

Shelby spent the next three days recuperating. Her ankle felt better each day, and she was now able to put weight on it while still using the crutches. Brandt and Cord took turns staying home with her, and even though she appreciated it, she felt the need to get out into the fresh air. Cord was currently in the kitchen making a pot of coffee. Retrieving her crutches, she carefully made her way to the back door, intending to sit out on the porch.

"Where do you think you're going?" Cord asked from behind her.

Shelby shrieked and wobbled from her startle. "Don't do that. You scared the shit out of me."

"I'm sorry, baby. I thought you heard me."

"Now, how would I do that? You and Brandt don't make any noise when you walk. Can you open the door? I need some fresh air."

"Okay, but you have to sit with your foot propped up." Cord moved around her and held the door open. Shelby cautiously moved toward the chairs. When she was seated, he pulled another chair closer and lifted her foot up to rest on it.

"Thanks."

"No problem, baby. Do you want a cup of tea?"

"Yes, please."

Cord went back inside to make her tea. He had just placed the drinks on the table beside her when she caught movement in her peripheral vision. Looking up across the yard, she froze in horror for one moment and then screamed Cord's name.

The noise she made wasn't enough to drown out the explosion, and she screamed again when Cord staggered back a couple of feet and landed on the deck. With tears streaming down her face, her heart nearly thumping out of her chest, she slid to the floor and crawled over to Cord.

His face was so pale and his eyes were closed. She took hold of his shoulder and shook him hard, calling out to him. Blood was seeping out of the wound near his shoulder and soaking his white shirt.

Shelby screamed again as rough hands grabbed the back of her shirt and hauled her to her feet. She tried to cling to Cord, but she was pulled away. She was shaking so much she could barely stand, and she shook even harder when the barrel of a gun was placed at her temple.

"Move, bitch," a voice spat near her ear. The rough hands began pulling her away. Shelby didn't dare turn her head, but the man moved alongside her and she saw his face in profile. It was the same face that she saw in her nightmares.

Shelby stumbled when her ankle nearly gave way, but Perez held her up by her shirt. She was sobbing uncontrollably, scared that Cord was dead. Perez didn't let up, just kept dragging her toward the front of the house, down the driveway, and out onto the street.

She looked around frantically, hoping to see someone she could call to for help, but there was no one. Cord and Brandt's property was on the outskirts of town on a huge tract of land, and the nearest neighbor was a mile away.

She cried out with pain when her foot landed on a rock and wrenched her already-injured ankle. She couldn't stop herself from falling to her knees. Ramone Perez pushed the barrel of his gun harder into her temple and bent closer toward her.

"Nothing you do is going to stop me. So get up or I'll shoot you now."

Shelby pushed to her feet and winced when pain shot through her ankle but clenched her teeth and began to limp toward the truck Perez guided her to. He shoved her into the passenger seat and wound his way around to the driver's side of the car. She cringed against the door when Perez got in and started the car. She prayed to God to save Cord.

* * * *

Cord moaned in pain and frowned when he couldn't work out what the persistent buzzing noise was. He couldn't remember where he was or why his shoulder was on fire. "Shelby!" he roared as memory slammed into him. Groaning with pain, he sat up and looked about as he reached for his cell phone. Ignoring the incoming text, he hit the speed dial for his brother.

"Brandt, I think Perez has Shelby. He snuck up on me and shot me. Call everyone in," he barked into the phone. "I have to get to the doctor's so he can patch me up."

"How bad are you hurt?" Brandt asked with concern.

"Shoulder wound. I think it's just a graze, but I hit my fucking head on the deck. Must have knocked me out for a bit. I'll meet you all at the doc's."

"I'll get Damon and his brothers to begin searching for Shelby. See you there. Hurry."

Cord raced to his truck and spun the wheels in the gravel when he planted his foot. Five minutes later he was inside the doctor's office, tucking his gun into the waistband of his jeans after Brandt handed it over. Luke and Sam rushed through the door as the doctor began inspecting his wound. Britt, Daniel, and the others who had promised to help keep their woman safe were on their phones via conference call, as they were still in transit. He flinched when the doctor disinfected the groove across his shoulder but listened as Luke spoke.

"We got a print off that stolen car. It was definitely Ramone Perez. I have an APB out on him, but we don't know what he's driving now. I was surprised he actually did his own dirty work instead of making one of his goons do it. That means he's desperate, and desperate men are dangerous. I'm hoping we get to him first, but our first and only priority is getting Shelby away from him safe and sound, so if any of you find her and can get her out safe, do it."

"Um, there is something I think you need to know," the doctor interrupted. "If you gentlemen would leave for a moment, I need to speak to my patient privately."

Everyone cleared the room, but the doctor detained Brandt before he could leave.

"I don't like to break patient confidentiality. In fact, I am totally against it, but I think under the circumstances you should know."

"What?" Cord barked impatiently. "Sorry."

"Don't apologize, the woman you love is in danger," the doctor conceded. "Shelby is pregnant."

Cord drew in a gasp of air and closed his eyes. When he opened them he pinned the doctor with his gaze.

"Are you sure? When did you do a test?"

"When she needed an X-ray, I had to ask if there was a possibility she could have conceived. I needed to take the necessary precautions to protect the fetus. She asked for a pregnancy test that same day."

"Fuck. We have to get her back, Cord. I love her so damn much."

"Thanks, Doc. Let's go."

Cord exited the room with Brandt at his heels. They entered the waiting room just as Luke finished a call on his cell.

"Okay, thanks. Keep me posted."

"Any news?" asked Cord.

"No. No one has spotted a man and woman traveling together in a vehicle, at least not the ones we're looking for."

"Have you got all the roads covered? Shit, they could be long gone. I have no idea how long I was out," Cord snapped with frustration.

"I have most of the roads in and out of Slick Rock covered, but there are only so many people I can call on."

Cord's cell phone vibrated. He looked at the screen, surprised to see Quin's number displayed.

"Yeah."

"Cord, I just saw Shelby pass by the garage in a car with a strange man. She looked scared. He was heading on the back road toward County Road Q1. Pierson is following but keeping out of sight. What's going on?"

Cord quickly explained and then cursed when he realized he should have brought the Badons in from the first. He trusted them, but they were so new to town that he wasn't accustomed to accounting for them in his plans.

"We'll come to your shop. Let us know if Pierson contacts you."

Within minutes, everyone had gathered at Badon Mechanics. Damon Osborne, Slick Rock's other sheriff, brought a large map of the area, which they spread out in the back office.

"Here's County Road Q1. It's my guess that Perez is aiming for the small ravines and canyons surrounding this area." Daman pointed on the map. "What sort of vehicle was he driving?"

"A four-by-four."

"Fuck. That means he could go anywhere off road. There are a lot of caves in this area. If it was me and I was planning to take someone out, I would do it here." Damon pointed again to a spot on the map slightly southeast of where they were.

"That looks like pretty rough terrain even for a truck," Luke commented.

"Yeah, but not impossible," Damon replied.

Quin's cell rang, interrupting the conversation. He put his phone on speaker.

"Quin, they've gone off road. I'm not familiar with the area, and it looks too rough for my truck," Pierson said.

"Tell me where you are. We're coming to meet you."

"Whoever is coming, make sure they have four-wheel drive. Bring the dirt bikes."

"Be there soon," Quin signed off.

"You have dirt bikes? Where are they?" Brandt asked anxiously.

"Out back. We were going to do some riding but haven't had the chance yet."

"Thank God, where are the keys?" Cord asked desperately. He wanted to be out there looking for Shelby and getting her away from Perez.

Grayson plucked two sets of keys from a board on the far wall of the workshop and tossed them to Cord and Brandt.

He and Cord headed immediately for the back door. "Wait," Damon called out. "You had better take these with you. I'm not sure how far the cell network reaches."

Cord accepted the police radios and handed one to Brandt. He fitted the key to the right bike on the first try and kick-started the engine. Brandt got on the other bike, and moments later they went fishtailing out of the lot onto the road.

Cord spotted Pierson sitting in his truck on the side of the road. He put his arm out the open window and pointed toward the line of trees off the left side of the tarmac. Cord gave him a wave of thanks. He applied the brakes and kicked back two gears, leaning over the handlebars of the bike as the terrain grew rough.

The urgency to get to Shelby was eating at him, and he was glad Brandt had handed over his .38, which was tucked into the waistband at the back of his jeans. He watched the ground, looking for tire tracks, and spotted them immediately.

Ten minutes later, he spotted the four-by-four just around a bend. He slid the bike to a stop, and Brandt pulled in alongside him.

"He's going to know we are here. He'll have heard us coming a mile away. The noise from the engines carries."

"I know, but we have to get to her, Brandt. Maybe one of us can distract him while the other creeps up on him."

"Okay, let's go. Keep your eyes open. He's probably on higher ground so he can see us coming."

Cord and Brandt made sure their cell phones were on silent and turned the volume of the police radios down. The last thing they needed was to alert Perez to how close they were getting if they found him.

"Footprints." Cord pointed. There were two sets in the sand. The larger prints fell steadily, indicating a man walking.

Cord's anxiety ratcheted up at the sight of the smaller prints. They were uneven, like a woman had been limping.

Cord took the lead, following the trail but watching his surroundings. Outcroppings of bare rock provided cover for them, but they could also hide Shelby or Perez. The footprints didn't veer off into a hiding place, though.

The trail led them unerringly toward a steep cliff face. The riverbed at its base was long since dry and filled with brush and boulders. As the ground grew rockier, the trail became patchy. Still they didn't sight Perez or Shelby.

Frantic with worry for the woman he loved, he halted at the base of the cliff and scanned upward. The back of his neck prickled, and his gut felt like it was full of lead. They were getting close. He always followed his instincts.

Using hand signals, he ordered Brandt to backtrack around the large boulders to cover him. Perez was so close that Cord could feel him practically breathing down his neck.

* * * *

Shelby was scared and in pain, but that all seemed so inconsequential after seeing Cord shot right before her eyes. There had been so much blood. She had been too shocked to look for the wound. Hunching against the passenger-side door, she thought she caught Quin looking at her strangely as Perez sped past their workshop. She tried to look back, but they were going too fast and Badon Mechanics was nearly already out of sight. Closing her eyes, she concentrated on how she had last seen Cord.

It had all happened so fast, and her body and mind had immediately gone into shock.

Shelby thought of the love she felt for her men and how they loved her in return. She hadn't even had the guts to tell them how she felt, and now she might never get that chance. Covering her stomach, she vowed to her baby she would do everything she could to get them both out of this alive. This was her chance at true happiness, and she wasn't going to let Perez take that away from her.

Perez slowed the vehicle and turned. He was taking them off road. *Shit. How the hell is anyone going to find me now? What if Cord is still unconscious or, God forbid, dead?* Perez drove for what seemed close to half an hour, as the going was slow over the rough terrain. Shelby asked herself where he might be taking her and why he hadn't just shot her back at the house, but her mind was blank. Finally, he stopped the vehicle. He'd held the gun pinned against the steering wheel, but now he pointed at her once more.

"Get out, and don't try anything or I'll put a bullet in you."

Shelby opened the door, but she answered, "As opposed to what?"

Girl, don't mouth off. But she knew he wanted to kill her, and she didn't understand why he was taking her out here instead of shooting her back at the house.

With courage she didn't know she had, she demanded, "Where are you taking me?"

"I lost six months of my life because of you. I could have lost a lot more than that. I'm glad I didn't run you down the other day. I've decided I want you to die slowly. Now get out!"

Perez shoved her, and Shelby tumbled off the passenger seat. She reached for the passenger door and bit her tongue hard enough to draw blood when her newly wrenched ankle threatened to give way beneath her as she tried to stand. She clutched at the door and breathed deeply, pushing the pain to the back of her mind. By the time she was back in control, Perez had walked around to her side of the truck.

"Move," he yelled, pushing the gun into her back.

Shelby let herself be guided, watching and waiting for an opportunity to escape. She knew she was no match in the strength department to Perez, because he had to weigh at least twice what she did, but if she found a way to get away from him, she wasn't going to waste it.

Only halfway up the side of a steep rock wall, Shelby cried out with pain as her ankle finally gave out. Grabbing onto a small bush, she tried to pull herself up, but the branch broke. Perez grabbed her arm in a bruising grip and half dragged her the rest of the way. Just below the top of the precipitous cliff was a small opening in the rock. Perez had to duck and nearly bend in half to enter, but he didn't stop or care as he hauled her behind him. He pushed her away from him roughly, and she landed on her hands and knees on the cave floor. Scrabbling to get as far away from him as she could, she hunched against one of the stone walls.

Shelby began to get angry. Angry for her parents and brother. Furious at how scared she had been because of this bastard and enraged at him for hurting Cord. If she was going to go down, then she was going to go down fighting.

Perez stood over her with the gun pointed at her, his finger around the trigger and an evil smile on his face.

Chapter Thirteen

Brandt kept back from the cliff face, sheltering behind some boulders while Cord investigated the open space before the cliff. They had worked together in the police force and now in security, and each knew how the other thought. Cord was placing himself out in the open, in danger, hoping to draw Perez out while Brandt provided cover, and he tried to locate the fucker the moment he stepped into view.

Keeping half an eye on Cord, he scanned the face of the cliff. Halfway up the cliff wall, Brandt spotted a small bush with a broken limb. Scrutinizing the spot, he let his eyes wander up and saw a small opening in the rock. Signaling Cord to get his attention, he pointed out the hole. Cord nodded that he'd seen it. There was nowhere else for Perez to hide. The shrubs and bushes weren't large enough to provide adequate cover.

Cord quickly made his way toward him to confer.

"I'm going to go up there. I think he'll stay put, but if he comes out and I'm only halfway up, I'll be a sitting duck."

"Let me go up, Cord. You're already hurt, and I can tell your shoulder's paining you," Brandt whispered.

"Yeah, but I'm high on adrenaline, so it's not too bad. It's better if I go. He probably thinks he killed me. Surprise is a good advantage. It will give the few extra moments I need."

"I'm not going to stay down here to cover you. I need to be closer for a decent shot, and I want to be there when we get to Shelby."

Brandt followed Cord up the steep slope, careful not to dislodge any of the smaller rocks and alert Perez to their presence. It took them longer than he would have liked to traverse the incline with such care.

They were only yards from the entrance when the echo of a gunshot resounded out of the cave.

Brandt roared with fear and fury and took off into the cave after Cord.

* * * *

Shelby whimpered with terror as Perez squeezed the trigger. She screamed when the gun exploded and waited for the pain. But it never came. Ramone stood over her, the gun smoking in his hand but the barrel aimed toward the roof above him. The bastard was playing with her.

A yell from outside made her turn her head toward the entrance of the cave, but then a low rumble made her look up. Perez lost his smile and tried to make a run for it, but he wasn't fast enough. The roof to the cave began to fall in.

Shelby huddled into a ball and prayed she wouldn't be crushed. A warm, heavy object landed on top of her, but she couldn't see what was happening. Dust in the air clogged her lungs, and the weight on top of her crushed her. Finally the horrific noise stopped and everything was quiet. She whimpered with fear when the body on top of her moved, and then warm hands grabbed her arms, pulling her up.

There was no light. The opening had been sealed, and she couldn't see who had her. She began scratching, slapping, and hitting out blindly until finally a familiar voice penetrated her shock and fear.

"Shh, baby, you're safe. We have you."

"Cord? Is that you?" she whispered hesitantly.

"Yeah, baby, I'm here. Brandt is, too."

"Perez. Oh God, he's got a gun."

"Shh, Shelby. It's okay, darlin'," Brandt crooned, and she heard him moving. Then she was sandwiched between her men, their love and warmth cocooning her. "Perez is dead. I saw the ceiling come down right on top of him."

"Oh good. I thought you were dead. Thank God you're alive," she sobbed, clutching at Cord's shirt. "Are you hurt badly?"

"No, baby, he just grazed me. I hit my head and got knocked out for a bit."

"There was so much blood, Cord." She sniffed. "Are you really all right?"

"I'm here, aren't I?"

"How are we going to get out of here? We're trapped."

"We'll be out sooner than you think, darlin'." Brandt wrapped his arm around her waist. "Everyone is coming to help look for you. I have a police radio I can use to call Luke to come dig us out."

"Tell him to hurry. I don't like being in here." Shelby began to cry, and Brandt pulled her back against him. "I hurt my ankle again. If he wasn't already dead, I'd take your gun and shoot him myself."

Shelby was shaking. Now that she was safe, the adrenaline in her system was looking for a way out. Brandt kept his arm wrapped around her from behind while he radioed Luke and the others for help. She leaned into Cord at her front, and he held her while she cried. Her tears slowed at about the time Brandt was giving Luke directions to the cave. Luke promised to get them out as quickly as possible, and she began to calm down.

Cord had propped her leg over his lap but kept her body close at his side so that she could snuggle with him. Brandt signed off with Luke and moved closer against her back.

"You okay, darlin'?"

"Yes. I am so tired, though. I don't know what's wrong with me. I can hardly keep my eyes open."

"Then don't try, Shelby. Close them and go to sleep. You never know, by the time you wake up, we might be able to walk out of here."

Shelby wanted to say that she hoped so. She wanted to tell them about the baby, but as the flood of adrenaline receded, she felt too exhausted to do anything but close her eyes.

* * * *

Brandt felt Shelby's body relax minutes later and knew she was asleep. Cord must have felt the tension leave her, too, because he eased away from them.

"Keep her warm. I'm going to see if I can move some of these rocks out of the way."

"I don't think that's such a good idea, Cord. It's so dark in here, I can't see my own hand in front of my face. You don't want to bring the rest of the ceiling down."

"I just can't stand leaving our rescue to others."

"There's not much you can do about it. I know how much you like to be in control, but sometimes you have to compromise."

"You aren't just talking about getting out of here, are you?" Cord asked quietly.

"No."

"Have I been that bad?"

"No. You've been more tolerant than I've ever seen you before. But I don't want you to push Shelby too far. We both know she has quite the temper on her, and I don't want her to end up walking away because you've pushed her beyond her limits."

"Don't you think she cares enough to stick around? She hasn't complained yet. The only time she has was about her car."

"And even though our intentions were honorable, we should have told her how bad her car was. Instead we took it upon ourselves to keep things from her. She had every right to blow up."

"Okay. You're right. I'll back off."

"Do you think she loves us? She hasn't even told us about the baby, and she found out days ago." Cord sounded worried.

"Yes, she loves us. I just don't think she's realized it yet."

"God, I wish she'd hurry up and tell us how she feels."

"I know. We just need to give her a little more time. She's had so much weight on her shoulders. Even though you were only grazed, she's going to blame herself. Our little girl is so caring, she puts everyone else before herself."

"And you think I'm a control freak," Cord said, and Brandt could hear the smile in his voice.

"Well, our life is definitely not going to be boring." Brandt chuckled quietly.

Luke's voice came over the radio. "Brandt, stay back from the entrance. We're about to start working our way in."

"Thanks, Luke, we'll be waiting."

Brandt and Cord listened as the men outside began working to set them free. They sat with Shelby cuddled up in between them, keeping her warm. Their rescuers had to meticulously remove the rocks and detritus from the cave entry bit by bit so they wouldn't cause another cave-in.

Three hours later, they had dug a hole large enough to admit sunlight. An hour after that, there was enough room for them to get out. Brandt gently woke Shelby, telling her it was time to go. He lifted her into his arms and carefully passed her through the opening to Luke.

As Brandt followed her out, he could hear Luke crooning to Shelby as he carried her down the incline.

"Easy there, little lady, you're safe now."

Cord followed him and moments later walked over to the paramedics, who had been on standby in case of injuries. After checking Shelby over, they pronounced her fit and well, besides having a badly sprained ankle with various abrasions, cuts, and bruises. The medics wrapped an ice pack around her ankle and cleaned her cuts.

Even though Shelby was covered in dirt with tear tracks making pathways down her cheeks and her hair in a wild halo about her head, to him she had never looked more beautiful. When the paramedics stood aside, Brandt leaned over and scooped her back up into his arms.

"God, Shelby, I love you so much. I was so scared when I found out Perez had taken you."

"I love you, Brandt," she said, hugging him tight. "I was so afraid to say those words back to you. Scared that he would win and take me from you. And then he did. The only thing I regretted was that I had never told you and Cord how I felt."

Shelby looked up and scanned the groups of men. She frowned when she couldn't find who she was clearly looking for.

"He's right behind you, darlin'." Turning around, he placed Shelby into Cord's waiting arms. He smiled as he watched Shelby hug his brother fiercely, and then she pulled back.

"I love you so much, Cord. I was so scared when he shot you. I thought he had killed you."

"I'm safe, baby. When I woke up and found you gone, my heart stopped in my chest. I thought I would die," Cord said in a voice so full of emotion that it rasped. Brandt could see the moisture in his brother's eyes.

He blinked back his own tears, walked closer to Shelby and his brother, and hugged them both.

"How about we get the hell out of here and go on home? I think we could all use a stiff drink and a shower."

"I would love to, but I shouldn't be drinking," Shelby replied quietly. "I'm having a baby."

Brandt exchanged a look with Cord and received a tiny nod from his brother.

"Sweetheart, we already know."

"The doctor wanted to make sure we knew when we went to rescue you," Cord added. "We're so happy, baby."

"I can't wait until your body rounds out as you grow our child. We are going to be with you every step of the way, Shelby. Never doubt it."

She blinked at them, astonished. "You already knew?"

Uh-oh. Brandt braced himself. "You're not mad, are you, darlin'?"

He was prepared for Shelby's fiery nature to assert itself, but she visibly relaxed. "I wanted to be the one to tell you, but I guess I'll get over it if we get married real soon. I want my baby to have her fathers' name."

Cord smiled slowly. "Are you asking us to propose, darlin'?"

"Yes." Shelby limped away from them and folded her arms across her chest. "Right now."

Brandt heard one of the paramedics chuckle nearby. He hadn't pictured himself proposing to their woman in the middle of a desert, all three of them covered in dirt, but Shelby's expression made it clear she wasn't taking no for an answer.

He met Cord's eye again. Moving as one, they dropped down to one knee. They each took one of Shelby's hands.

Together, they asked, "Will you marry us?"

Tears filled her eyes, and her face was overcome with a beautiful smile. "Yes, I will."

Brandt was back on his feet in a heartbeat. He held Shelby and felt Cord press against her back. They surrounded her with their love.

Brandt felt his face split wide. Even though they had already known Shelby was pregnant, she had finally let go to trust them with her heart, body, and soul.

Chapter Fourteen

Shelby was looking forward to tonight so much. The doctor had given her the all clear. Her ankle was one hundred percent healed and her baby was doing fine, and that meant one thing. Brandt and Cord hadn't made love to her since she had first been injured and had made it clear that they wouldn't risk hurting her. For weeks she had imagined how she would seduce them once she had healed.

Brandt had accompanied her to the doctor's office, as he wanted to make sure the baby was all right after her ordeal. Even though she had the paramedics check her over once she was out of the cave, he and Cord had been a little concerned. She could now tell by the smile on his face he was feeling more relaxed.

"Are you ready to go, darlin'?"

"Yes. We're done here. Am I going to be able to go back to work now?"

"Sure, if that's what you want, Shelby."

"Oh, I do. I've been going a little stir-crazy at having to stay home."

"We noticed." Brandt laughed.

"Can we drop by and see Cord before we head home?"

"Uh, Cord was going to come home for lunch today. He was going to bring something from the diner."

Shelby held in her laughter. She could see from the heat in Brandt's eyes that he wanted to make love to her, and since Cord never came home for lunch she suspected that her two fiancés had plans of their own. He helped her into his truck and hurried around to the driver's side.

"That sounds nice," she replied, glancing at her watch. "But since it's only eleven and Cord doesn't break for lunch until one, that gives us two hours to kill. What are we going to do to occupy ourselves?"

"You are a little minx. You know damn well I've already sent a text to Cord. He's probably already halfway home."

"God, I hope so." Shelby groaned as she crossed her legs, trying to relieve the ache in her clit.

"Hold that thought, darlin'," Brandt rasped and turned out of the parking lot.

They made it home in record time, and for once Shelby was glad not to have seen the two sheriffs, or Brandt might have received a ticket. Pulling up close to the steps, he helped her down from the truck and into the kitchen.

Cord was leaning against the counter sipping a mug of coffee. He perused the length of her body and gave her a heated look. Shelby glanced down to his crotch. *Oh yeah, he's raring to go.* She didn't need to look at Brandt, since she'd already seen how hard he was during the ride over.

"How did your appointment go, baby?"

"Well, since you're here and ready for me, I suspect you already know the answer to that, big boy." Shelby sauntered up to Cord, putting an extra sway in her hips, and cupped his hard cock.

Cord closed his eyes, pushed his hips further into her hand, and groaned. "You are so going to get it, baby."

"Promise?" she asked sassily.

"Oh yeah." Cord moved quickly, picked her up, and then raced out of the kitchen and down the hall. He lowered her feet to the floor, and between him and Brandt, they had her naked in seconds.

"On the bed, darlin'," Brandt commanded.

Shelby kept her eyes on Cord and Brandt as she climbed up onto the bed. They had begun to undress, and she didn't want to miss a thing. Her men peeled off their clothes so fast it was a wonder they didn't shred them.

"You are both so beautiful. I have never seen such handsome, sexy men, and I can't believe you're all mine."

"Believe it, baby. And you're all ours." Cord got on the bed, lay down beside her, and pulled her into his arms, staring deeply into her eyes. "I love you, Shelby."

"I love you, Cord. Now make love with me." She turned her head to look at Brandt as he got on the bed behind her. "I love you, Brandt."

"Me, too, darlin'. Now just lie back and feel. We are gonna make you feel so good."

Brandt leaned over her shoulder and kissed her. His kiss was hot, wet, and wild, like he couldn't get enough of her taste. He slowly withdrew until he was sipping at her lips and then kissed his way down the side of her neck and across her shoulder.

Cord turned her head back to him and took her mouth with a kiss so carnal and erotic that her pussy clenched and opened, begging to be filled. His tongue was everywhere, sweeping the insides of her cheeks, over her teeth, and up to tickle the roof of her mouth before finally coming back to slide along hers.

When he pulled away, they were both panting for breath, and he eased her from her side to her back. "I want to eat you all up, baby. I crave the taste of your skin." He paused to lick across the top of her breast and then lave his tongue over a nipple. "Mmm, so sweet," he murmured before sucking her nipple into his mouth.

Shelby moaned as electrical pulses zinged from her breast down to her pussy, causing more cream to leak out. She cried out when Brandt leaned over her and took her other breast into his mouth. She arched up into their touch. Brandt scraped his teeth over her hardened nub, suckled her again, and then released her with a pop.

"You are so fucking responsive, darlin'. I love the little sounds you make. Don't ever hold back, Shelby," Brandt said in a voice breathless with need. He then leaned down to her breast once more.

Cord kissed his way down her body, stopping whenever he found one of her erogenous zones and giving it more attention. He smoothed his hands up and down the insides of her thighs, gently parting her legs. Then he settled in between them. Shelby moaned at the first lick, and Cord responded with a growl. Sliding his tongue up and down her moisture-coated folds, he bestowed pleasure upon pleasure on her.

Moving his arms, he wrapped them around her legs and with one hand parted her labial lips. Cord flicked his tongue over her clit, starting off slow and increasing the pace with every pass. Shelby sobbed with pleasure and nearly screamed when Brandt sucked one nipple while pinching the other. He bent down and began to talk in her ear.

"You are gorgeous, darlin'. Cord wants you to come in his mouth, Shelby. Don't hold back. Give him what he wants."

Shelby mewled when Cord released her labia and lifted his mouth away from her cunt. When he thrust two fingers into her sheath, she cried out.

"Come for me, baby. Let me drink down your juices," he rumbled out.

Closing her eyes, she gave herself over to her men. Cord pumped his digits in and out of her pussy while laving his tongue over her clit, and Brandt sucked on her nipple. She was bombarded with sensation after sensation and knew it wouldn't be long before she climaxed. Then Cord twisted his fingers inside her and slid them over her G-spot. Bucking her hips up, she screamed as great waves of pleasure washed over her. Her pussy continually contracted and released around Cord's fingers as he sucked on her clit. Just as she thought the waves were over, he moved his digits in a curling motion and sent her into another orgasm.

When the pulses finally stopped, Shelby felt totally boneless and gasped for air.

"So fucking sexy. Your cum is delicious, baby," Cord panted. "Roll her over."

Brandt helped Shelby to roll back on her side and cuddled her from behind. She could feel his erection against her ass, so she wiggled her hips and pushed back into his cock. Cord lay down at her front, leaned in, and kissed her. His mouth brought the embers of her desire from glowing to flaming in seconds.

"We are going to love you together, baby. I want you to relax and let us do all the work." Cord pulled her leg up over his hips and began to knead her breasts.

"A little cold, darlin'," Brandt said just before lubricated fingers slid between her crack. He took his time, letting her get used to having his fingers at her back entrance, and when she relaxed he pushed a finger into her anus. Shelby moaned and reached out for Cord. He slid a hand down to her pussy and lightly massaged her clit.

"That's it, baby. Let Brandt prepare you. We are going to make you fly so high, Shelby."

"I have two fingers in now, darlin'. I just need to get one more in, and then you'll be ready."

Brandt suited action to words and pushed another finger into her rectum. Shelby sobbed as the bite of burning pain enhanced her pleasure.

"Good girl. She's ready."

She felt the blunt head of Brandt's cock at her back hole and tried to relax. As he pushed in, she pushed out, and they both groaned when the head of his cock popped through the tight muscles of her sphincter.

"Fuck. So tight," Brandt groaned. "You okay, darlin'?"

Shelby was incapable of speech so just nodded. Cord was still massaging her clit, and that sensation combined with the feel of Brandt pushing into her ass had her on the brink again.

"She's so close. I can feel every ripple around my dick. Her ass squeezes so tight," Brandt gasped. "Okay, I'm in."

When Brandt pulled her leg off Cord and lifted it high into the air, it caused her to clench on his hard cock. She moaned and pushed back against him, wanting to feel more of him. It felt so erotic to have his shaft shoved up her ass but so wickedly pleasurable. Cord shifted closer, and she looked down to see him holding the base of his penis.

"Keep your eyes on me, baby. I want to make sure we don't hurt you."

"You won't. Come inside me, Cord. Please? I need you both so much."

Cord began to push his cock into her pussy, and even though she wanted to close her eyes at the exquisite pleasure, she kept them open and on Cord.

"You are so wet, baby. And so fucking tight," Cord moaned. "Give me some room, Brandt."

Brandt pulled his cock back a little as Cord pushed forward, and she whimpered with pleasure. He didn't stop until he was in her pussy balls-deep. Cord withdrew partly, and as he thrust forward, Brandt pulled back. They set up a rhythm of advance and retreat, push and pull, making sure she was full of at least one cock.

She could feel the tension building into something bigger than she'd experienced before. Her men were now sliding their cocks in and out of her holes with fast thrusts, and Shelby felt the warm tingles gathering in her womb. Molten lava spread from her core out to her legs and into her pussy. She gripped their cocks tighter and tighter until all of a sudden the tension snapped.

Shelby screamed as she was hurtled into climax, her muscles contracting and pulsing as her pussy leaked her cum.

Brandt's cock expanded in her ass, and then he was yelling as he shot cum into her ass. Moments later, Cord roared, and she felt his cock jerking as he, too, shot her pussy full of semen.

Her men ran their hands over her body, gently soothing her from her climactic high as they cuddled with her.

Shelby smiled, grunting when Brandt withdrew from her ass and patted her cheek. He was back soon and cleaned her up with a warm washcloth.

"I should get up and shower." Shelby yawned.

"Why not just take a nap, baby? We have a busy day tomorrow, and you'll appreciate the rest."

"What are we doing tomorrow?" she asked with a smile, lifting her heavy eyelids to look at Cord.

"You already know, don't you, minx?" He gave her a chagrined smile.

"How the hell do you always find out what we're up to, darlin'?"

"Don't you know that women have eyes in the back of their heads," she replied sassily.

"Ha. Rest up, Shelby. We have a wedding to attend tomorrow."

"You're definitely gonna keep us on our toes for the next fifty years or so, aren't you, baby?" asked Cord.

Shelby cuddled up to Cord with a happy sigh. "Looking forward to it."

And so were they, if the love in their eyes and the smiles on their faces were any indication.

THE END

WWW.BECCAVAN-EROTICROMANCE.COM

ABOUT THE AUTHOR

My name is Becca Van. I live in Australia with my wonderful hubby of many years, as well as my two children.

I read my first romance, which I found in the school library, at the age of thirteen and haven't stopped reading them since. It is so wonderful to know that love is still alive and strong when there seems to be so much conflict in the world.

I dreamed of writing my own book one day but, unfortunately, didn't follow my dream for many years. But once I started I knew writing was what I wanted to continue doing.

I love to escape from the world and curl up with a good romance, to see how the characters unfold and conflict is dealt with. I have read many books and love all facets of the romance genre, from historical to erotic romance. I am a sucker for a happy ending.

For all titles by Becca Van, please visit
www.bookstrand.com/becca-van

Siren Publishing, Inc.
www.SirenPublishing.com

CPSIA information can be obtained at www.ICGtesting.com
Printed in the USA
LVOW04s1959300315

432595LV00023B/749/P